The
Foley
Artist

The
Foley
Artist

STORIES

Ricco
Villanueva Siasoco

Published by Gaudy Boy LLC,
an imprint of Singapore Unbound
www.singaporeunbound.org/gaudyboy
New York

For more information on ordering books, contact jkoh@singaporeunbound.org.

ISBN 978-0-9828142-6-0

Cover design by Flora Chan
Interior design by Christina Newhard

In memory of my parents
Alita and Amado

Contents

In my desire to be Nude
I clothed myself in fire:—
Burned down my walls, my roof,
Burned all these down.
                    —*José García Villa*

We're all born naked and the rest is drag.
                    —*RuPaul*

The
Foley
Artist

STORIES

The Rice Bowl

Viva wants her boobs back. Viva—real name Victor—is seated on the zebra skin toilet cover, whining in a high falsetto at Barbarella, a linebacker of a drag queen. Viva says, "Barbie, give me that bra"; "Barbie, you ain't got no right"; "Barbie, you best watch your ass or I'll sic G. I. Joe on it." Barbie (a nickname that Barbarella—real name Barry—hates) applies her Peach Perfection eyeliner in the mirror and says, "Stop flapping them gums, honey. I'm catching cold."

Viva's homemade "Thunder Bra" is really an old T-shirt that she has carefully, artfully, sewn into the perky C cups of a Wonderbra. Barbarella has borrowed them for the third time this week, strapped them over her wide, hairy chest, beneath her black kimono. In Des Moines there's only one decent lingerie store for a respectable queen to patronize—Victoria's Secret, on the second level of Jordan Creek Mall—and it's all the way on the west side of town, in the tony suburbs (formerly oat fields). Eleven point five miles from The Rice Bowl, and neither Viva

nor Barbarella—divas who gleam like windows after a rain—
owns a car.

Everyone in Des Moines knows The Rice Bowl: how "four-
star" our food is; our location on the South Side, just outside
the wrought iron gates of the fairgrounds; and most important
(and here I speak with affection), the kind of girls who work
here. Viva once said to a curious reviewer from *The Des Moines
Register*, "Baby, don't you know a glamour-puss when you see
one?" Barbarella leaned on her shoulder and added, "We're just
a couple of Twinkies: yellow on the outside, white and dreamy
on the inside." The reviewer ate his cashew chicken as sweat
formed under his armpits. Barbarella is Filipino; Viva, Chinese,
like me. I'm not a drag queen. I'm just gay. When I ask the girls
to do something, wipe down the booths or set a table for a party
of six, they give me a hard time, call me "Double Happiness" (my
real name is David), or something they think is equally sassy. But
taking shit from the two of them doesn't bother me; it's part of
the manager's job. My father, Louie Chen, opened The Rice Bowl
in the winter of 1969, after he had immigrated to the States with
his wife. Mom had accepted a fellowship in civil engineering at
Iowa State, and sometimes Dad, in his I-Am-Funny-Immigrant
mode, jokes with the regulars that I was a "gift" from the university. He and Mom were always kidding around like that
before she split with a physics professor and moved to Southern
California.

Even without her, The Rice Bowl is thriving. As I see it,
there are three reasons for our success. *Number One:* we don't
pretend to be something we're not. *Number Two:* we've got the
best damn spareribs in town—the kind that melts off the little
finger bones when you bite into them, unlike the radioactive

things The Other Mr. Chen serves at China Palace, a few blocks down on East 14th Street. But most important, *Number Three:* Viva and Barbarella, our only waitresses (they prefer to be called *entertainers*), are a big draw. The *Register* reviewer compared them to beauty queens: "Except Viva's hips are more slender," he wrote, "and Barbarella looks like she has hockey pads for shoulders."

Des Moines is a little backwards, but not as unwelcoming for a gay person as you might think. I mean, there is one gay bar, The Garden. That's where I met my boyfriend, Howard—a lanky, somewhat bookish, mealy-haired teacher at West Des Moines High School. Viva calls Howard "The King of Square," but his nerdiness and his endless chattering about quantum things and mathematics (he teaches Algebra II and geometry) are exactly what I find attractive. When he bought me a drink that first night when I was celebrating my twenty-fifth birthday, it was his black horn-rimmed glasses that caught my eye, his scraggly, unshaven jaw. Even now I love the way he cocks his head when he's puzzled, like a dog. Too bad he's lived here his whole life and is ready to call this city quits.

Des Moines definitely has its quirks: this obsession with skywalks (Viva calls them "big glass penises"), countless shopping malls (two Lane Bryants for every fat housewife in the city), and endless ribbons of farmland on which, lately, eighteen-hole golf courses and miles of gated communities have begun to appear. Howard's school was built a couple of years ago out past the airport, on a ploughed-over field that once harvested soybeans and corn instead of hormonal teens. "Sprawl is taking over America," he proclaimed to Viva the other day, "Des Moines is doomed." His green eyes glinted maniacally and his hands curled into talons. Viva just puckered up and gave him her trademark figure-Z snap, before sashaying into the kitchen. She thinks if Howard wasn't a teacher, he'd be writing conspiracy theories in some carbon-copied newsletter. But Viva has demented visions of her own.

Viva's delusions have to do with the endless blight on August called the Iowa State Fair. It's the largest of its kind in the Midwest, and people drive their boxy mobile homes hundreds of miles to see god-awful attractions like Elsie the Cow, a six-hundred-pound butter sculpture with an udder that squirts milk. To top it all off, over Labor Day weekend, live on the Kum 'N' Go Main Stage, there's entertainment by every smiling swing choir in the state. Now that, by golly, is entertainment. Viva wants the three of us to enter the talent show this year (the cash prize is a thousand dollars) and lip-sync Diana Ross's all-time greatest hit, "I'm Coming Out." I think it's a bad idea and tell her so. Viva, however, has stars in her wily eyes. One morning while setting tables, she unveils her name for our singing trio: Asian Slaw. Barbarella loses it, her blue pageboy tilting on her head.

Howard and the regulars think the girls are a crack-up. One Friday morning near the beginning of June, Mr. Henry asks Barbarella out on a date. Old Mr. Henry, a retired librarian, was my father's first customer when he and Mom opened The Rice Bowl decades ago. Every day he appears in our doorway, beneath Dad's eight-sided mirror, dressed in these bright suspenders that clash with his purple fedora. Once he asked Dad if he had any candles lying around to celebrate his twenty years of collecting Social Security! The old guy is alright, though he calls whoever waits on him (including me) *girlie*. Maybe he got the habit from Dad, who sometimes sits with him and reads the Chinese newspaper. Mr. Henry eats his lunch at 10:30 each morning, at the round six-top next to the swinging kitchen doors, and calls out to whoever's nearby, "Girlie, you're keeping an old man waiting!" He orders the same lunch special (No. 36): egg drop soup, egg foo young with pork, and on the side, no-ice iced tea. He likes Barbarella the best. Her tips from the old geezer are twice as much as Viva's or mine.

So when Mr. Henry asks her out, the crazy Filipino girl says yes. Viva whispers to me, "Where the hell they gonna go, Val Lanes for a couple games of Rock 'N' Bowl?" Later, I close the door to the little girl's room while Barbarella is changing into a crushed velvet number that clings to her huge frame like a wetsuit. "That old geezer really thinks you're a girl," I say. "He'd knock you silly if he knew you played football at East High!" But she won't listen, just keeps penciling in her eyebrows and powdering the blotchy temples above her eyes. "Doesn't matter if he thinks I'm the Queen of Sheba," she says, "He asked, and I'm going." I pinch her arm and let the bathroom door latch.

The next morning after their date, her round, made-up face is glowing, her nails done in a bright shade of purple with silver glittering stars. She tells us that she and Mr. Henry are going to run off together, to some remote island in the Caribbean. "We're in love," she says, refilling small hourglass bottles with soy sauce. "He's my rumpled old prince."

Viva plops in the booth opposite Barbarella and scowls, tearing the wrapper off a pair of wooden chopsticks. "Barbie, you're a fool," she says. "You gonna give that geezer an angina."

*

There's a new restaurant opening in the old Subway shop, The Other Mr. Chen stops in to tell us. "My daughter," he says, his hair wispy like the brim of a straw hat, "she works at Home Depot and talked to construction men. They buy three chandeliers and wall-to-wall carpeting!"

The Other Mr. Chen pumps his arms over his head like a cheerleader. He and Dad never talk business, kind of like how my father and I don't talk about Howard. It's not that my father isn't accepting of my sexuality; we just haven't made an after-school special of it. I consider Dad's comfort with Viva and Barbarella as proof that he's okay with The Wide, Wide World of Gays. Howard thinks I should push him more, but I think Howard's had too much diversity training.

Dad says to The Other Mr. Chen, "South Side cannot support another Chinese restaurant. No one better than Rice Bowl!" The Other Mr. Chen slams his fist on the counter. My father quickly appends his comment—he can't bear to hurt Mr. Chen's (or anyone's) feelings—with "I mean, The Rice Bowl and China Palace the best," though we both know China Palace is a dive that serves mediocre food to run-off customers from the T.J.Maxx next door. Of course, no one mentions that other restaurant—Grand China—which pulls in twice as much business as our restaurants combined. But Grand China caters to a different crowd—rich insurance men and their sparkly families near Jordan Creek Mall. Once I treated Dad to a birthday dinner there—fresh boiled lobster, Peking duck, taro root ice cream. Dad could only obsess over the wholesale price of the lobster and the cost of washing the linen napkins every day. Grand China strikes me as the Amazon of Chinese restaurants: vast and dependable, but in a different league from our mom-and-pop market. On the other hand, another Chinese joint in our neighborhood is definite cause for worry.

After The Other Mr. Chen leaves, Dad calls everyone together in the kitchen for an emergency meeting. Everyone: Viva and Barbarella, me, and Mauricio, our Brazilian cook. Mauricio is as old as or older than Dad, and sometimes they argue like a married couple. *Shape Up,* Dad announces, is our new motto for The Rice Bowl. Shape up our tables, shape up our service, shape up the way the girls talk to his customers. I flinch; it's the first time I can remember him referring to his customers in the possessive. When he finishes his speech, he walks past the bathrooms to the back stoop (he calls it his "office") to smoke a Pall Mall. The screen door creaks.

Viva turns to Barbarella and, within earshot, says, "Who woke Richard Simmons-san up on the wrong side of the bed?"

*

We're slammed on Saturday afternoon. Dads dressed in L.L.Bean fishing vests are fighting with their kids and ordering broccoli chicken in bulk. Pushy, mud-cleated brats are screaming for cheeseburgers, and then are disappointed with the way Mauricio cooks them—boiled, on white bread. I'm covering three of Viva's tables and manning the register up front, and I can hear Dad in the kitchen screaming at Mauricio in Mandarin (God knows why, because he barely understands English) about running out of water chestnuts.

Dad storms through the swinging door holding a withered cabbage. Is he headed outside for a smoke? I catch him accidentally whacking a toddler in a high chair and I hurry over to the kid, offering apologies to the parents. Then Viva, who has been MIA for most of lunch service, comes up behind me and whispers that I'm needed in the back. I give her a look—*Now?*—and when she responds with a shrug of the shoulders, I follow her to the kitchen.

Under a rack of hanging pots, Barbarella is seated on the rice bin in tears. Mauricio is at the stove ignoring her. Dad walks in, still holding the wilted cabbage, and then he takes her leather order book away. He places her manicured hand in his; it looks like he's going to propose.

"What's wrong, girlie?" he asks, and for a second it's like the dining room on the other side of the swinging door is empty, the screaming game-show families silenced, the tornado of forgotten side orders and tinkling silverware stilled—for just one Brady family moment—as my father pulls himself onto the wooden bin and wraps his arm around Barbarella's shoulders.

"He's gone," Barbarella says, dotting her thick mascaraed lashes with her finger. Dad's short legs dangle next to her stockinged ones. If there's one thing I've learned in my twenty-eight years at The Rice Bowl, it's that whatever catastrophe happens here, whatever crisis (financial, personal, weather-related) befalls us, it seems to find a natural balance in Dad's goodwill.

"He wasn't even man enough to dump me," Barbarella whimpers. "This morning I walked by China Palace and there he was, sitting at that round table in the window. And he saw me, too, I know he did, Louie! But he looked down in his egg drop soup like he was embarrassed to even say hello!"

I lift a metal spatula from the counter and scrape crusted egg off it with my fingernail. Maybe Mr. Henry led her on. Howard thinks he had slept with Barbarella, and then told her whatever she wanted to keep her big mouth shut. Despite what I said earlier, being gay in Des Moines isn't total sunshine. At times it's like being a Buddhist in Salt Lake City.

Dad lifts Barbarella's chin and looks her in the eye. "You don't need him," he says, smoothing her blue pageboy wig, "You are beautiful woman."

"Mr. Henry no good for business, anyway," he adds, "Always hanging around, ordering refills with no ice!" Barbarella chuckles. Viva offers her a high-five.

My father stands, tottering on the rice bin, and sticks his tongue out at the customers on the other side of the order window. Then he leans down and kisses Barbarella on her head.

Mauricio screams at us to get out of his kitchen. Dad jumps to the floor. "Now, shape up, girlies!" he says, banking the cabbage off the rim of the garbage can. "Hungry Rice Bowl customers waiting!"

*

The plate glass window of the Subway shop is being soaped in white circles, and if you stand across East 14th Street it resembles the scales of a fish. Every morning as we walk by, Dad makes a face like he's caught a whiff of rotten bok choy and tells me (as if it's some kind of epiphany), "David, a new restaurant is moving in! A new restaurant is moving in!" The Other Mr. Chen, formerly Dad's Number One Enemy, stops by our place regularly, he and my father sipping tea from handleless cups while the rest of us wipe down the vinyl booths. He's become as permanent a fixture as Old Mr. Henry, who has stopped eating at both The Rice Bowl and China Palace altogether. Mr. Chen's daughter has been snooping around, and in July she learned that the landlord of the shop leased it to a company called Wok Express.

"A franchise!" The Other Mr. Chen says to my dad, "Who can compete with large businesses?" They look like a couple of old women in a Terrace Hill mansion, complaining about the subdivided Victorians and all of the Brazilians and Vietnamese moving in. For the rest of the day, I work on soothing my father, telling him that competition is good for us: market share, supply and demand, basic stuff I learned in business school.

"Besides," I say to him, "it'll separate our loyal customers from the rest."

That evening I give Mauricio fifty bucks to take Dad to Prairie Meadows to gamble on the greyhounds. It's a warm night in July, not too humid, and my father loves the smell of mulch at the track. Mauricio pulls Dad out the screen door, my father yelling, "Lock all doors and do not forget to bring the drawer home!" (It seems the worst practice to me, but after all these years he still refuses to buy a safe.) If my father had his way, he'd open and close the restaurant seven days a week. But because of his backaches, Dr. Leavitt forced him to cut his seventy-hour week in half.

Viva is at the apogee of her State Fair obsession. Tonight she's ranting louder than the obnoxious DJ, who promises "all hits, all the time" from the boombox in the order window. I'm counting ten-dollar bills, and force myself to block her out and concentrate on my task. But all Viva can talk about is the livestock exhibition—*the cows! the heifers! the bovines!*—while Barbarella mocks her roommate's obsession. "Double Happiness," she says to me, "you would not believe our apartment. We've got hundreds of stuffed cows in the goddamn bathroom!"

Viva gives Barbarella a shove and changes the subject to the fried dough she loves, the sticky cotton candy (as if I've never had any myself), and the hot guys who set up the yellow tents. "Those ripped T-shirts and tight jeans," Viva says, snapping her figure-Z. She turns and walks to the little girl's room. Through the open door, I can see her adjusting her boobs so that they're level. "Mister Trade Boy!" she leans out and yells to Barbarella. "I've got your rice cakes over here!"

Barbarella shrugs and joins her in the room. I know she's still fresh from Mr. Henry's rejection by the way her makeup is only half done: real eyelashes instead of fake ones; no scarf around her neck hiding her Adam's apple. The register receipts that Dad had printed are a mess, and it takes me a good half hour longer than it should to write my reports. From my table in the middle of the dining room, I listen to the girls weighing alternatives for the evening—fart around with the closet homos at The Garden all night or rent *White Squall* for the zillionth night in a row. The radio emits a low static hum, and I barely notice when it stops and the cassette deck is opened. When I glance up, a white glove appears in the window, gently replacing the boom box on the counter. Suddenly, the high-pitched voice of Diana Ross, fuzzy and somewhat canned, bounces off the framed prints of pork dumplings and lo mein adorning our walls.

"I'm coming out!" Viva sings with Diana Ross, pointing at me with a long white glove and parading between two banquet tables. She's wearing an immaculate frilled Shirley Temple dress and shouting, "I want Des Moines to know, got to let it show!"

Barbarella emerges from the little girl's room, equally decked out in a (size 12?) silver-threaded kimono. "I'm coming out!" she belts. Her big hands are on her waist: "I want the boys to know! Got to let it show!"

I stare down at my reports and imagine one of those long canes yanking them out the back door. Soon their arms are wrapped around each other like two beige-skinned queens straight out of *Rocky Horror*. Their free hands grip imaginary microphones to their lips and their screeching is joined by a dog outside.

The trumpets and drumline crescendo and then, thankfully, fade. Barbarella stands behind Viva and holds her at the waist, both of them bowing deeply in front of me. I repeat my mantra: "I'm not doing the diva bit. Louie would have a shit fit," though I'm not sure he really would. I stack the money into piles of ones, fives, tens, and twenties. Howard would probably ask: If wearing a dress did upset my dad, would that be a bad thing?

Viva smooths her ruffled dress and calls me "Double Grumpiness." She and Barbarella turn their backs and shuffle to the little girl's room. I grab the bills, zip them into a bank pouch, and place it in my backpack. "Let's go to The Garden," I call out, "my treat."

*

After Viva and Barbarella untuck from their kimonos into jeans and frilled blouses, Howard honks his horn and drives us to The Garden, tapping the steering wheel and singing along to the Indigo Girls. The Garden is located in a former grain storage warehouse in the old business district skirting the state capitol. The business district is really block upon rundown block of boarded-up storefronts, dilapidated copy places, and fenced-in lots. All the big businesses in Des Moines, Traveler's Insurance and The Meredith Corporation and NCR, have moved out west, to these suburbs built of pink-hued concrete, with town officials who have managed to hide not only the trash but the old people and minorities as well. Howard says the young couples who live out there have identical McMansions that look large enough to hold Mass.

Before I quit community college—where I knew more about operating a business than any of my economics professors—I wanted to become one of those suburban types. But then the goal became sort of meaningless (Barbarella would say it was the day Mom ditched us), as generic as the fortune in a fortune cookie. What I really want is something less tangible: to make my father happy. Me and The Rice Bowl have been his only loves, and I want him to retire in the next few years. I want him to see the aunts and uncles he left when he emigrated from China. I've always been curious about China. Maybe we could travel through Beijing and the provinces for a couple months. But would Howard come, too? I told Barbarella the other night that if I had one wish, I'd move with Dad to someplace truly exotic (Vermont or Oregon would do) and become one of those personal chefs who work for outrageously wealthy people. You know, Oprah or Bill Gates. Who couldn't use a good-looking guy like me dishing up spareribs and fried rice?

When we arrive at The Garden, Viva cups her hand like royalty and waves at her friends in a corner table. She and Barbarella immediately desert us. Howard pulls out a stool for me at the bar. "It's gonna be a Wok Express," I say as he removes his jacket, "The chains are slowly moving in."

I order a sloe gin fizz from the cute redheaded kid who just moved here from Boston. Howard doesn't know it but last Thursday, after too much vodka and a 2 a.m. last call, the redhead and I went home together. In the front seat of his Honda, I went down on him as he told me his name, Chad Kline. Later, in his bedroom, both of us shirtless and slumped on a futon on the linoleum floor, I felt his perfect six-pack, teasing him. *Abs are signs of obsessive behavior,* I said. He shrugged and said he used to wrestle.

Now Chad disappears behind a jagged row of liquor bottles. "It could be a good thing," Howard says, sipping his Diet Pepsi. "You know, David vs. Goliath. It's a chance for you to drum up some free publicity. You can use this to show Des Moines how corporate America is crushing mom-and-pop businesses like The Rice Bowl!" He's getting excited, as if he's explaining one of his algebra proofs, gesturing with his lanky arms.

I glance across the room at Viva, who's holding her arms in the air like Evita. She shimmies her chest for the applause of her friends, only a few of whom are in drag tonight, doing Bette and Cher to earn a few extra bucks. Howard touches my arm and I spin my stool, our knees touching. "Do you really think anyone gives a shit about us? The newspapers want funny stories about Viva and Barbarella, but nobody would notice if The Rice Bowl burned to the ground."

Howard wants me to quit the restaurant and move to Chicago. There's a lot more opportunity, he says—he could get a job in the education department at one of the museums or at a magnet school in the larger districts. "We could get an apartment in Lincoln Park; you could start a catering business or something." I nod. The idea of moving to a new city just to reestablish distributors, stump for clients, spend my day hiring and firing a bunch of inexperienced cater waiters? No, thank you. Chad sets my sloe gin fizz on the bar with one of his freckled smiles.

What would I do differently in Chicago? After his "Shape Up" talk the other day, I sat with my father on the back stoop of the restaurant. He told me that he'd willed The Rice Bowl to me. It was one of those weird Kodak moments, not because of the revelation, but because his death was something I'd never thought about. Besides his recent backaches and some minor arthritis in the wrists, my father will live until he's 150. It may sound cheeseball, but I want to keep The Rice Bowl, this thing that he built from scratch, lucrative and alive.

I sip my drink and lie, say to Howard that Chicago is a great idea. I don't want to fight. He eats a handful of almonds from a shot glass on the bar. "I've got some money saved," he says. "It's enough to get us set up. We can be partners: Howard and David's Catering."

"You want to start a tab?" Chad asks, dimples fast at work. I remember removing his black T-shirt, his boxers, running my lips along the thin trail of hair from his belly button to his penis. Howard doesn't have a clue. I, on the other hand, know about his indiscretions—Barbarella has seen him here alone and told me he'd picked up a farm boy on the dance floor.

Howard orders another Diet Pepsi, then turns to watch Viva. Chad squirts pop into his glass from a blue nozzle, staring at me. Not a hard stare like he's cruising, but with a soft focus, as if to ask, *How about it?* I look away. Barbarella is dancing, her blue wig bumping into a disco ball. When I swivel back to the bar, Chad has tucked a piece of paper under some napkins and I read it when Howard isn't looking. In lowercase letters it says, *Later?*

Viva comes up and holds my knees. "Barbarella has officially agreed to be my costar," she says. This is not news. "That only leaves room for one more entertainer." She touches the tip of my nose and I push her hand away.

"There is no way I'm making a fool of myself in front of Greater Des Moines." Howard—ever the instigator—leans into Viva and whispers, "I think David's scared of commitment."

I sigh. "I'd like to see *you* in a gold lamé dress."

"Why not?" Howard says, chugging his Diet Pepsi. "I'm not afraid of making a fool of myself. Viva, count me in."

She kisses him on the cheek, leaving a red mark next to his five o'clock shadow. "Honey, we'll make a glamour-puss out of you yet!" Then she pinches my tricep and gestures with her chin to Howard. "Your boyfriend's gonna drive those pretty little math students out of their heads."

They small-talk and giggle about the fair. I catch Chad's attention and point at my empty glass. He nods. With him, I know I barely have to say a word.

*

It's after 3 a.m. when Chad drops me at home. Louie's asleep on his burgundy La-Z-Boy and a handful of crumpled tickets litter the coffee table. "Dad, go to bed," I whisper, lifting his elbow. Since he was left behind, my father's routine consists of opening the restaurant, closing the restaurant, and then coming home to watch the Weather Channel with a six-pack of Sapporo beer. It makes me feel helpless and paternal to see him like this, a button left in a dresser drawer.

I guide him to his bedroom and remove his food-stained sneakers and pants. "The Rice Bowl the best," he mutters. "Number one in all of Des Moines." I ease him under the blanket and his mumbles become snores. This is important to my father—that The Rice Bowl not only succeed, but be the best. Funny, because it was originally Mom's idea to open a restaurant. My father wanted to be an astronomer. The other night I discovered him on the back porch, a bottle of Sapporo in hand, gazing at the star-besotted sky. On the bamboo calendars he prints every year for advertising, he includes an astronomical calendar with a black-and-white moon in its various states of undress. I'm sure he never came to America to cook Chinese food; Mom was the one with the business savvy. She kept our books. When she left, I had to quit school and take over.

In my room I collapse on my single bed, arms behind my head, staring at the white ceiling. With the lights on it's too bright. I stand up again and flip them off. It's hard not to imagine the restaurant scene in Chicago as better than Des Moines's! Outside the window, a motorcycle revs its engine and pulls away. It strikes me that Howard's offer is a lot like Mom's offer to Dad all those years ago in China. Why did he follow her around the world?

Dad's snoring filters through the drywall separating our rooms. In the stark moonlight, the shadows of objects—a chair, a shelf, the coat rack in the corner—divide the room like the front page of a newspaper. Sometimes Dad's snoring comes through the wall like a radio wave and wakes me, and I believe we're in the same room. Maybe I should have stayed at Howard's apartment tonight; he'd asked. But Howard always asks. I said I'd take a cab home with the girls, and when The Garden closed, I went with Chad to his apartment.

In the morning, my father pokes his head into my room. I roll away from him and yank the pillow over my head. I hear the click of the light switch. "Shape up, David!" he says, "Rice Bowl get the reporters today!"

*

The opening of the Iowa State Fair always brings a slew of television people to The Rice Bowl, ordering rounds of coffee and leaving bad tips, stuffing fried wontons down their gullets, regressing to teenagers in a high school cafeteria. We're located right across from the media gate. White vans with TV logos and towering antennas line both sides of East 14th. In our nine booths, half a dozen guys dressed in bush vests accompanied by blonde-haired reporters in dress suits gossip and primp. Viva and Barbarella carry trays of steaming food over their heads, bitching at the camera guys for leaving their equipment in the aisle. "Sweetie, that ain't the kind of pole I want in my face," Viva says to a stocky man near the kitchen. He laughs, then winks at his table of friends.

My father and The Other Mr. Chen have banded together against Wok Express. We've printed expensive books with coupons for free spareribs or a dessert with any meal. On the back cover, a huge, winking moonface (Dad's idea) says, SUPPORT YOUR LOCAL BUSINESSES!!!, and yesterday I hired some responsible-looking kids from the neighborhood to pass them out at the gates.

Howard and the girls have been practicing their routine in his apartment after the restaurant closes. Barbarella is sewing a miniskirt for him to wear, and last night he careened around the living room in Viva's heels, knocking over a flower vase and a stack of ungraded essays. I don't think he's been that off-balance or vulnerable his entire life.

Howard has told me that if they win the talent show, he'll put his share of the thousand dollars toward a deposit on our house. He's trying to sell me on the moving-in-together idea. I listen carefully, wonder if his performance with Viva and Barbarella is a way of proving something to me. Whether in Chicago or (he's now decided) Des Moines, he wants us to live together. Near The Rice Bowl, if necessary, and near my father on the South Side.

Dad's talking up The Rice Bowl to a short, balding news anchor seated below a photo of the Great Wall. The bald anchor looks amused and when I clear the table, his is the only plate that's clean. "Human interest!" Dad says finally, pulling Viva over to them. "You talk to this girlie. She give you good sound bite."

"Or good something," Barbarella adds, passing their table. Viva ignores her, smoothing her satin kimono.

"We'll see, Louie," the bald anchorman says, shaking my father's hand. He tells his crew to pack up their equipment, and walks across the street to the fair.

*

Barbarella is going to wear Viva's Thunder Bra. Tonight, with her blessing. It's a humid, mosquito-ridden night before Labor Day and I sit in the grandstands with my father and The Other

Mr. Chen. Maybe a hundred people—a few actually sporting mesh tank tops—crowd the fairground's metal bleachers. Overweight, sunburned, white-trashy moms and dads, chowing down on footlongs and blue cotton candy.

A sickly-looking spotlight scans the stage and lands on Viva, face tilted toward the green and purple flags drooping above the stage. She looks shorter than usual, a five-foot munchkin in her frilly gown and arm-length gloves. Her orange wig is piled high on her head like a turban. The gigantic speakers framing either side of the stage emit a buzz that's more static than sound, and when Viva opens her mouth the voice of Diana Ross exclaims:

I'M!

COMING!

OUT!

A lone guitar riffs from the speaker on the right. Trumpets from the left, and then drums building under Diana Ross's voice. Viva struts to center stage and a man next to me, wearing a Budweiser hard hat (with plastic can holders and a long snaking straw), places two fingers in his mouth and whistles in that anonymous, crowd-like way.

Barbarella and Howard, dressed in tight polyester miniskirts, black scoop-necks, and long gloves to match Viva's, appear from the right and strut across the stage, hands on their hips. A chorus of backup singers blasts at rock-concert volume, Barbarella and Howard mouthing the lyrics. I notice two svelte women with backpacks below me, bobbing their heads to the disco beat.

Howard is still shaky in Viva's heels, but when the three of them form a row and do that supermodel strut they've been rehearsing, I can tell he's hit his mark. The crowd suddenly cheers, like the greeting of a studio audience. The women with the backpacks are laughing (the tall one raises an arm in the air and cheers), and then they begin to clap with the rest of the crowd to the music, the young kids beside them screaming that they're coming out in unison. There's more whistling and Beatles-like screaming and Howard and the girls, onstage, are flashing white, white grins. I can't remember the last time I've seen Howard truly enjoying himself (besides ogling houses in gated communities) since we started dating more than two years ago.

When their act ends, Howard and the girls curtsy, the crowd stomping rhythmically on the metal bleachers. Even from a dozen rows back, I can see them sweating. Howard's grin is larger than Viva's or Barbarella's and he shades his eyes from the harsh stage lights. I doubt he can see me but I wave.

*

Dad's balding anchorman snubs us after the talent show, but a pink-suited reporter does a feature on Viva, Barbarella, and Howard for the ten o'clock news. A harmonica player from Council Bluffs took first place, but, as always, Viva and Barbarella provide the more interesting story. For her part, Viva is her siren self. She gushes about her new singing gig at The Garden, finally managing to put in a plug for The Rice Bowl. The chipper, long-legged reporter pulls the microphone away from Viva and asks what sets us apart from the fast-food chains down the block.

"It's about the love, Sugar," she says, raising one of her penciled eyebrows at the camera, "or else it's just soggy old pork on a plate." She's using that long-lashed, Streisand voice of hers. "Isn't that what everybody wants? A little bit of love?"

The reporter smiles, turns to the camera, and signs off by stating her name and location. Viva leans in and mugs for the camera.

Dad taps me on the shoulder and points at Howard who wobbles unsteadily toward us in his tight miniskirt, a pair of lycra biking shorts showing beneath. He looks endearing and ridiculous. Dad mutters, "Howard make one ugly girl," and we laugh.

*

We drive to Howard's favorite suburb, Grassy Day, after an impromptu celebration at The Rice Bowl. On the sixteen-inch TV above the cash register, Viva's interview had been edited to a few sound bites about the difficulty of wearing heels, keeping her hair from frizzing in the hot weather, and then a brief shot of Howard and the girls framed in the round spotlight. No mention of Viva's singing gig or The Rice Bowl. Dad scowled and Mauricio waved his metal spatula at the TV. The girls ditched us altogether to gloat (unperturbed) to their friends at The Garden, and Dad told me to take the rest of the night off.

Now, speeding down I-80, just Howard and me, the headlights of his pickup catch green signs before they whiz by, spelling out what we're nearing, and how far away. The All-Hits Station is paying tribute to eighties music, a parade of songs by bands with cute, alliterative names like Culture Club and Duran Duran.

We drive past the granite birdbath that marks the entrance to Grassy Day. On the radio, Boy George sings about Karma Chameleon. *You come and go, you come and go-o-o-oh.* "What the hell is this song about?" I ask, but Howard isn't amused. He turns off the radio and stares at me. "Are you sleeping with somebody?"

Where's this coming from? Did Viva tell him about Chad Kline? "Huh?" I ask, playing it cool, fiddling with the radio knob.

He reaches for my hand and holds it still. "David, I'm asking you a question. Have you been screwing around?" He pulls up on the gearshift and parks his pickup in front of an unfinished house, this huge skeleton of two-by-fours, exposed staircases leading nowhere, and one or two low-pitched roof beams. It looks like a ribcage or an architect's model, something scraped raw and built of Tinkertoys instead of wood.

"Would it matter to you?"

"Of course it would," Howard says. He's wearing that look of pity he gets when he thinks that I'm lying. "We're talking about our relationship."

But I hate talking about our relationship. Or cheesy things like commitment. Howard is a romantic; he loves Valentine's Day and stray animals and Internet cards that play musical greetings. There's a sitcom-gone-serious quality to it all that makes me cringe. Why don't we talk more about the things we hate: how we sometimes despise the same people we love? How come no one ever wants to talk about that?

"There isn't anybody," I say.

"David."

"Yeah?"

"Viva told me about that redheaded kid." He cocks his head, waiting.

"And what did Viva say?"

"She said you seduced him."

"Come on, Howard."

He stares through the grimy front window. Dirt is caked around the edge of the windshield, and I imagine a pair of giant binoculars. "Viva said you went to his apartment that night after The Garden."

A bunch of teenagers, joyriding in a compact car, scream at us as they speed past. Sheets of newspaper float down the street in their wake. I don't want to lie to Howard, but I also don't want to confess; I'm too much of a wuss for that.

He touches me on the forearm. "I don't care if you did, David. It's just sex. It doesn't mean anything." I want to ask him about his cheating, who he's picked up at The Garden, but this, too, seems pointless to me, to accuse each other, slam fists on the dashboard and fight. What would happen if I told him about Chad? Would we break up? I don't want to be alone. After one of their late-night rehearsals in Howard's apartment, Barbarella told me how lucky I was. "Howard is exactly the opposite of other guys," she said. "Mr. Henry wouldn't show his emotions for all the iced tea in the world."

Howard clears his throat. "Those guys," he says, "they don't matter." There's a soft rasp in his voice. I turn and stare at the unfinished house. Some kind of animal is sending sawdust up from the floor, a raccoon or a stray cat—something small on four legs. It moves with its belly close to the ground, then jumps up the stairs and disappears.

We sit in silence. "Are you ready?" I say at last. Howard doesn't reply, just turns the key in the ignition and pulls away.

A mile or two from the entrance to Grassy Day, the ranch houses with their bright picture windows begin to thin out, separated by blocks of new construction. I place my hand on

Howard's thigh. His jeans feel scratchy and rough. I wonder if he's still wearing those smooth biking shorts beneath.

Howard's pickup is the only car on the street. If you drive far enough into this subdivision, the ranch houses disappear completely and the only sight is acres and acres of undeveloped lots. I've never told Howard, but this is my favorite part—the paved roads dotted with street lamps, the empty lots uncluttered with houses or crops or people. Howard turns on the radio again and Cyndi Lauper sings "Time After Time" in her grating, Betty Boop voice. Howard covers my hand on his thigh with his own. I wonder if there's another exit in this direction, but I don't ask. I don't want to know.

Deaf Mute

Nancy had said the best fish and pork were sold five blocks from the Cathedral of the Immaculate Conception, so Noel Borgos followed his mother, his Tito Vic, and his teenage cousins Nancy and Claudine as they weaved through the wet, narrow aisles of the markets at Baclaran. Every so often a stray cat, thin and sickly, scavenging the rot left in the alleys, would dart from beneath a display of cheap handbags, splash in a puddle at his feet, and disappear across the aisle.

Noel wiped sweat from his forehead with his shirt sleeve. "How much farther is it?" he asked. Nancy rolled her eyes. She was a slender girl who wore her long black hair in braids and, like Noel, was entering her last year of high school.

"It's behind the Pizza Hut. *Naku,* you whine a lot."

He walked beneath a blue tarp shading a display of bolo knives. He hated his cousin's smugness. Nancy was less confident than pushy, he decided, like the pretty girls at his high school. He recognized her defensiveness in so many of the

Filipinos he'd met here in Manila. A few paces ahead, Nancy wrapped her arm around her sister's waist. Claudine—shorter and heavier than Nancy, with a thick melon-y face and horn-rimmed glasses—leaned in with her hip. She whispered to her sister and they laughed.

In the middle of the aisle his Tito Vic made a deep guttural sound at Teresa, Noel's mother, and they waved at a dainty woman across from them. His uncle was deaf, and he signed to his sister with sharp, tossing gestures, as if he were discarding unwanted items—spent lottery tickets or orange peels—on the ground. His mother looked back at him and smiled.

Noel followed his relatives past a long row of vendors selling bolts of fabric displayed on end like crayons in small boxes. The crowded market was difficult to navigate, and from every booth voices shouted for attention in Tagalog. It was both exotic and strangely familiar, and it seemed to Noel to typify Manila in mid-July. Here he was, his first trip outside the US sandwiched into his brief summer vacation. Before he had arrived here with his mother, he had imagined swaying palm trees, white-sand beaches, and grilled tuna steaks served with mango salsa. That was what he had hoped for and what his single mother, on her meager income, could not provide—fine dining and expensive resorts that his private school friends, whose parents were rich white doctors or technology entrepreneurs, enjoyed. Now that he had lived in the hard grip of Manila for a week, he had begun to realize how his notions had been flawed: he had always pictured Filipino objects, never people. The reality of this place was, more than anything else, throngs and throngs of homogeneous people. Brown arms, brown faces, hair wiry as his own and dark as the Charles

River at night. Pausing beside a vendor hawking Chiclets and fragrant sampaguita necklaces, he watched his mother and Tito Vic bargain with strangers across the aisle. Vic pointed at a leather belt looped around a high bar, while his mother counted peso bills and sniped at her brother in Tagalog. He watched them indifferently, waiting for the end of the boring documentary. Other Filipinos clamored around his mother for the attention of the vendor. Noel felt ordinary. In Boston there were other Asian kids, of course, but not in these multitudes. Here, he thought, touching a carved bolo on the table, he looked exactly like everyone else. No white kids around to provide contrast or fill the space around him like Styrofoam peanuts.

His mother purchased the leather belt for Tito Vic and trotted ahead. Noel hurried to catch up to her.

"Do you know where we're going?" he asked.

Teresa scowled, "I lived here for thirty years, Noel. I haven't lost all of my memory."

She approached a fat, bearded vendor behind a table of dead fish. Melting ice dripped from the corners of the table into the street.

Nancy stood behind Noel and leaned collegially on his shoulder. "Tatay doesn't like to serve guests seafood. He thinks it is dirty."

"Then why's he letting Mom buy it?"

"He can't control her anymore. She's too American now." Nancy pulled her sister to them. They hovered on either side of him, breathing lightly on his neck.

"Tita Teresa says Daddy always used to smell like fish," Claudine added. "She called him her little *bangus.*"

In the shadow of another canopy, his mother and Tito Vic argued with the fishmonger. "Bangus?" he said, not looking at his cousins.

"Milkfish," laughed Claudine. "Don't you know any Tagalog?"

He smiled. His cousins reached around him and locked hands. Nancy pulled her portly young sister away and they ran up to his mother and pointed to a spade-headed squid. Tito Vic whined, his lean arms crossed over his chest. Teresa nodded quickly at the vendor. The man reached across the table with great puffing noises, wrapping both the fresh bangus and the squid in the front page of the *Philippine Daily Inquirer*.

Tito Vic walked up to Noel and tugged at his sleeve. He signed angrily, making stunted nasal sounds, but Noel didn't understand.

*

"Why do you call Tito Vic a *deaf mute*, Mom? Isn't it just deaf?"

She looked at him as if he'd uttered an obscenity.

"That is just what we called them, *deaf mutes*. It's not meant negatively."

Teresa zipped her clear makeup bag and placed it on a stained narra bench at the foot of Nancy and Claudine's bed. Noel tipped his chair against the wall of the girls' bedroom, which they had cleaned and vacated for Noel and his mother.

"But Tito Vic's not mute, Mom. He can speak—sort of."

"*Ay*, Noel. Don't ask so many questions."

Had he upset her? He knew his mother could sulk for days without saying a word, until he left a kitchen drawer open or a lid unscrewed and then she would explode at him in a sudden rage. Lately he had taken her moodiness as opportunity for sinking into his daydreams about Chad Kline, the red-haired boy on his wrestling team. Chad had recently moved to Boston from a suburb in Los Angeles. Some mornings, if his house was still asleep, Noel touched himself under the sheets, imagining the curves of the red-haired boy, until he came. Then he would join his mother and his sister, Maribel, for breakfast in the kitchen. Except for a loose bed joint, he tried to be as quiet as possible in his room. He never knew if they heard him. One of his nightmares was that his mother would find the T-shirt he hid under the mattress for cleaning himself after he masturbated.

Now, his mother slipped through the thin mosquito net covering the bed and lay down. She rested her palm dramatically on her forehead, her elbow pointed in the air.

Noel dragged a chair to the window and pulled his MP3 player from its case. He wrapped the ear-hook headphones around the back of his head, watching the bumper-to-bumper jeepneys along Roxas Boulevard, their passengers squatting in the bed of the old military trucks. In the middle of the boulevard a tricycle taxi with plastic streamers attached to its antenna inched for space. Noel closed his eyes and tried to feel the deep bass line of his music over the blaring horns and people outside. He felt far from home. In their triple-decker back in Cambridge, little more than a week ago, he had set up a hand-picked stereo system with surround sound and an expensive CD player that held five hundred CDs. He sat on the floor of their living room, listening to the speakers mounted from the corners of the ceiling. He'd saved up for a year to buy the stereo. His mother was packing a huge cardboard box with the word *Balikbayan* printed in angled letters on four sides. She was dwarfed by the box.

His mother was a small woman—a Keebler elf, his brother-in-law, Thomas, joked—with dark, permed hair and a certain aloofness toward waiters and cashiers that embarrassed him. When he shopped at Filene's Basement with his mother and Maribel, a clerk would inevitably say to the petite women, "You must be sisters," and they would laugh and wave, as if it was the first time they'd ever heard the joke. On the thin Oriental rug in their living room, Teresa arranged items for the balikbayan box: softball-shaped eggs containing pantyhose, dozens of bargain bin lipsticks, reflective pencils, twelve-ounce bags of M&M's.

"Why are you packing all this crap?" Noel asked.

"It's not crap! This is *pasalubong.*"

"For who?"

His mother scowled, opening a package of pastel-colored M&M's and putting him to work. Noel divided the chocolate candy into Ziploc bags while his mother wrote the names of his relatives on pieces of masking tape, sticking one on each plastic bag. The handwritten tags seemed as formal and generic as "Hello, My Name Is" badges.

"This pasalubong is for Tito Vic and his girls. They love knickknacks from the States. It is a tradition."

Filipinos had never struck Noel as people with tradition. The large Brazilian family that lived in the triple-decker across the street, sure, but Filipinos? His mother and her girlfriends made greasy egg rolls or deviled eggs and held potlucks to which they dragged their families on Thanksgiving and the Fourth of July. At those occasions they laughed at the same Tagalog jokes until dusk settled on them like a fine mist and Noel was called to set kerosene lamps on the shaky railing of the Borgos' front porch.

The smell of jeepney exhaust and fried bananas on Roxas Boulevard repulsed him. Noel removed his wrap-around earphones and stood in Tito Vic's second-floor window. What was Chad doing right now? It was exactly twelve hours' difference in Boston, and he imagined Chad holding a wine cooler to his lips, at a pool party maybe, talking to his friends about boring jobs. Why had his mother forced him to come?

She snored loudly under the mosquito net. Nancy and Claudine shared this bed, as had Tito Vic and his mother years ago in the same dilapidated room. Was one bed cheaper than two, or was this familiarity another Filipino thing that he didn't understand? Noel parted the thin net and sat on the mattress. He felt tired in this heat and noise from the boulevard.

He closed his eyes and dozed. A few minutes later, Claudine knocked on the open door. "Tatay asked for your assistance in the garden. Are you asleep?"

Noel sighed. His mother rolled onto her stomach and mumbled for him to go. It was one of her tests, he knew. Either he heeded her wish or added to her long list of impertinences. *What my father always taught us,* she repeated when she was angry at him, *was to respect your elders.* And then she would smile, unable to remain angry. "You and your sister are spoiled by this country. When you were born, the doctor turned you over and stamped 'Made in the USA' on your *powet.*"

Noel got up, tied the laces of his ragged sneakers, and followed Claudine down the back stairs to the garden.

*

The numbers were easiest to understand. When Tito Vic held out his hand and counted backward from three, both men lifted the heavy oil drum in the middle of the garden and carried it to an alley outside Vic's glass-sharded walls.

Noel liked his uncle. He was small and cagey, like his mother (Noel, on the other hand, was tall and studied, with careful gestures and an often-embarrassed face). Tito Vic also had a child-like whimsy that Noel admired. Once, unprovoked, he yelped at an orange blimp in the sky. When Noel's cousins opened their umbrellas and complained of the relentless heat, he tickled them until the two girls laughed. Sometimes he punched his Army friends in the arm. He guessed Vic was in his early fifties, a few years younger than his mother, and he knew his uncle had manicured lawns at the Manila Country Club ever since his wife had left him a dozen years earlier. Nancy was the one who had kept Teresa Borgos apprised of her brother's life and managed the house when her mother left. Tito Vic was also stubborn; he possessed the same proud chin, the same tight-lipped smile, as his mother and their seven siblings, who seemed to stare at Noel from old photographs in the family's crumbling Spanish-style villa.

Now his uncle stood in a narrow sluice between hedges and motioned for Noel to come closer. He placed his hands on the young man's shoulders and pointed to a withered bush.

"Pull it out?" Noel asked, mock-pulling the bush with two hands.

His uncle shook his hands *no* and grimaced. He crouched down and lifted a long branch. On the tip was a single, dried-out leaf, brittle and yellow on the underside. Noel was hot. He wanted to lie down.

"You want me to water it, Tito?"

Vic grabbed the boy by the wrist and pulled him down to him. Noel looked closely at the tiny leaf, to the spot where Tito Vic pointed a dirty fingernail. At the fork of the branch, a delicate green bud was just beginning to emerge. Tito Vic held onto his wrist, staring in his eyes. So the bud was rejuvenating at the end. Was he supposed to praise his uncle's work?

His mother called to him from an upper window. Tito Vic gave him a friendly push, and Noel ran up the stairs and joined his mother in the bedroom. As he pulled off his sweaty T-shirt and changed into a clean one, his mother scolded him from beneath the mosquito net. "He was trying to explain his ideas for the garden, Noel. You just didn't hear him."

*

In Tito Vic's humid kitchen, the whirring of electric fans—one slotted into the windowsill and one in the long cement hall—and Nancy's quiet knife-chopping made the afternoon feel languid and soft. Noel sat at the round plastic table and ate pork rinds, watching Priscilla, the family's maid, stir a cast-iron pot on the stove. Behind her, Claudine labored over the sink, scaling his mother's bangus. In the way Claudine pressed Priscilla's arm to pass by her, he sensed the girl's affection for the age-spotted maid—and conversely, Priscilla's independence. His mother had told him that Priscilla had been with them since his Lolo and Lola—Noel's grandparents—had given birth to Vic. Then Teresa recalled a tearful Priscilla on the day she had left for the airport, Priscilla holding a bag of floury polvorón candy for her during her long journey to the States.

Noel had never met his Lolo or Lola. Unlike Nancy and Claudine, elderly people were oddities to him, as disparate from his experience as a warm evening in December. But Nancy and Claudine were at ease with this old woman, and Noel felt suddenly ashamed of the crisp new Levi's he'd planned to sell his young cousins for a profit.

Tito Vic, bare-chested, banged on the flimsy screen door. He'd been working in the clumpy garden the rest of the afternoon, and his tank top hung from his pants pocket like a dishrag. With a sharp cry he yelled at Claudine, who found a juice glass and filled it with water for her father. His uncle drank noisily. When he was finished, he handed her the glass (she was waiting), and signed brusquely to her. Noel thought he was beginning to recognize patterns, certain motions that kept recurring in his uncle's gestures.

Claudine frowned. She held the glass in her right hand. "But Tita Teresa asked—"

Her father hit her squarely across the cheek, the empty glass shattering as it hit the floor. Tito Vic scowled as he pushed the squeaky door open and returned to his garden.

Nancy quickly moved to her sister, crouching in front of the refrigerator. Noel watched as his cousins picked up the large shards scattered on the floor. He wanted to be with his friends on the other side of the world, watching a horror flick like *Night of Desire* in the cool, lava-lamp glow of his room.

"No fish," Claudine whispered to Priscilla, who stood over the girls. She nodded, removing a frozen pork rump from the freezer above their heads. She seemed to avoid Noel's gaze, as if to meet his eyes would be to acknowledge his notion that she'd witnessed all of this before.

*

Noel felt sticky and strung out after their dinner of roast lechon, steaming sinigang soup without the bangus, and leche flan that his mother had made with extra custard and served chilled from the refrigerator. In the second-floor bathroom, which reminded Noel of a highway rest stop because of its cinder-block walls and high, unscreened window, he turned on the water heater attached to the tub. Nancy had taught him how to operate the boxy contraption on the first day he had arrived.

Noel stood beside the tub and listened to the heater groan to life. He hadn't mentioned Tito Vic's violence to his mother, the crack of his hand on Claudine's cheek. Was this normal? His mother had never laid a hand on him or his sister Maribel (except in affection, of course), and he wondered how this small, deaf man and his mother could have been raised by the same parents.

Cats mewed outside the high window. Naked, his teeth flossed, Noel climbed on top of the toilet seat and held onto the bottom of the sill. He peered out into the quiet clay yard where his mother, his Tito Vic, and their seven brothers and sisters had once played, imagining not a *merienda* of RC Cola and garlic peanuts, but his young titos and titas playing Hide and Go Seek or chasing one another under the clothesline. No, not Hide and Go Seek—Kick the Can. He had no idea what they had played, really. They were frozen in his mind as adults, had never been seventeen or applying to colleges, or been in love with a red-haired boy on the wrestling team and clueless about a career, much less the contents of the next day. He wondered if Chad Kline was sleeping in—it was Saturday morning in Boston—or wide awake, figuring out how to waste another vacation day.

The cat's feet clicked on the shed's tin roof. Noel counted the row of spindly camachile trees growing along the side of the shed. With a graceful leap, the cat jumped down and strode across the patio toward the house. Noel heard the fast, hollow clucking of a tongue.

When he raised himself on his toes, Noel saw his Tito Vic crouched on the stoop below, waving a chunk of bangus in the air. The emaciated cat was just a few feet from him, and when it made its move Tito Vic pulled the piece away and ate it, taunting the stray with delight.

Nicolette
and Maribel

Nicolette was used to questions: asking for directions, respond-
ing at job interviews, answering her perky placement counselor
or the immigration officer with chunky black glasses whom she
met once a month at a federal building in Post Office Square. She
had only lived in Boston for five months but her life seemed a
long list of questions. *What's the snow like?* her sister, Menchie,
asked when she called long-distance from Manila. *Do you have a
boyfriend? A job? When are you going to buy a car?* So when her
classmate, a Filipino-American woman named Maribel, inter-
viewed her in sign language class, Nicolette sighed, answering
with one-word replies.

"Where are you from?" Maribel asked.

Nicolette spelled *Manila* with her fingers.

"What do you do?"

"Nurse."

"Favorite TV show?"

"No TV."

Nicolette covered her mouth and yawned. She'd been up since six that morning, reading the last chapter of a romance novel she had borrowed from the public library. She glanced at the clock and noted a half hour left of class.

"Do you have a boyfriend?"

Nicolette signed "Men are," and then let out a small howl. Maribel laughed. The class turned to the two women as Franklin, their instructor, tried to settle the group down.

*

Nicolette was a coarse, big-boned girl with spiky black hair and a pursed-lip smile that often masked a scowl. Her classmate, Maribel, was as bubbly as Nicolette was cynical. Maribel was also eight months pregnant.

Following the class, Nicolette paused outside the white brick building. Tall lamps cast scallops of light on the parking lot and lit the dozen or so cars as if they were on display. From the east, a cool autumn breeze brushed Nicolette's skirt and chilled her under her thin sweater. She was thinking of home—not her basement studio in Brookline, but her real home in Manila, and the joy of driving her Subaru on a night like this beside the bay. She unclicked her purse and removed a pack of cigarettes. There was a solitude to the night that she preferred.

Maribel joined her on the steps. "When I first saw you, I knew you were Filipino. Guess how?"

Nicolette pumped her lighter, cupping it to the cigarette at her lips. She shrugged.

"My mom pointed it out to me. It's the button nose!"

She watched the pregnant woman gather her waist-length hair behind her and tie it into a ponytail. It reminded her of her own hair, before she had had it cropped. Maribel's face was round and shiny, a polished plate, and her gestures seemed animated: a marionette's. After several minutes of small talk she even popped, as if someone had yanked invisible strings attached to her elbows and knees. "Shit," Maribel said, holding Nicolette's arm. "I'm late for meeting my husband. It was nice to meet you—I like the way you talk."

The way she talked? Nicolette thought her accent was undetectable. The night was cooling quickly and she took another drag of her cigarette before stubbing it beneath her white sneaker. Beyond the parking lot, she watched Maribel rush past the diamond-holed fence. Even this far along in her pregnancy, the woman wore heels. Nicolette remembered her American cousins who'd visited her in Manila. Like Maribel, they possessed this same blithe manner, this same hurry to the next item on a punch list. And these cousins were lazy—their English was less precise than hers, cluttered with idioms and unnecessary slang. When her ex-boyfriend, Peter, met them, he would imitate their perky voices: "So whadda you guys do for fun?" *Americans and their corny slang,* she thought.

She walked to the T station, deciding that she would not sabotage the possibility of friendship. So far Nicolette had avoided making friends, reading as much as time afforded (both her romance novels and the *New England Journal of Medicine*) in the opulent reading room of the Boston Public Library. Once a week she allowed herself to break from her studies and her temp work and lounged on the grassy Esplanade beside the Charles

River, contemplating the numbered sailboats in the bay. She carried orphaned women's magazines that she salvaged from the laundromat with her because they, more than anything, seemed to echo her feelings about her new life: *The Modern Woman Speaks: Career First, Spouses Second. What Makes a Place Home?* One Sunday afternoon a nervous voice interrupted her reading, and she looked up from her Nora Roberts novel to see a good-looking black man with his black Labrador retriever, stooping to ask directions. Nicolette looked at him impassively, making it clear that he was an interruption. Other times on the Esplanade, her sister, Menchie, or other *kaibigan* in the Philippines interrupted her thoughts, and she would then remove the Date Due card from the back of her library book and compose a list of twenty-five things to share with them about her quiet life in the States.

Still, her ability to organize—to sort her relationships into neat compartments like supplies in a medical closet—frustrated her. Seated on her bench beneath the wide, cloudless bay, she would never admit that she longed for the messy logistics of a man. She could manage everything else—her career, her apartment, the demands of family and ex-boyfriends back home—but she could not will love into her life.

*

The following week, though she'd told herself to be pleasant, she pretended not to notice Maribel, who sat in the desk behind her eating an apple.

Franklin greeted the class with a sloppy jumble of signs, making them understand that they were to spell their name and their favorite food. He was a paunchy, thirty-ish man with unkempt hair and wire spectacles. He was chronically late for class. Still, Nicolette thought he dressed like the smart boys from her nursing college, and she liked the gentle snap of a pistachio shell in his teeth, which he pried open as he observed her classmates in small groups. Tonight, after elaborating on his favorite food, Franklin explained the next assignment: in pairs, they would sign each other's biography.

"I know, interviews again," he said, his boyish voice a surprise after thirty minutes of silence. He distributed a handout on blue paper. "But let your partner get to know you. Open up a bit, have some fun." He winked at Nicolette as he handed her the assignment sheet and then dismissed the restless group of adults.

"I think he has a thing for you," Maribel whispered to Nicolette.

Nicolette closed her purse, turned, and smiled at Maribel. The pregnant woman seemed less done up than the previous week, in a dark Lycra dress that accentuated her small breasts and large stomach.

"I'm sorry?"

"Franklin. I think he's got a crush on you. See how he stares? *Cosmo* says that you can tell if a man's interested by watching his eyes."

Nicolette said that she hadn't noticed. She hated that Maribel quoted the same magazine she read each month. Following class, the women sipped decaffeinated coffee from a vending machine and agreed to work together on the assignment. Maribel invited Nicolette to interview her over dinner that evening; her husband, Thomas, was working late, coaching his wrestling team. "I'll make you my famous Cobb salad," Maribel said. Nicolette suggested they cook adobo or another heartier dish instead. She didn't have a kitchen in her studio apartment and wanted to take advantage of Maribel's invitation.

Maribel grimaced. "Thomas doesn't like Filipino food. He thinks it smells up the house." They sat with their steaming coffee on the pyramid of steps leading to the school's front door. Kids playing kickball screamed from an adjoining field.

"We'll just use a little garlic. Let your husband suffer."

"I don't know, Nicolette."

"This assignment . . ." Nicolette said, running a hand through her spiky hair. She stopped to consider. "How about a compromise? Fried rice and Cobb salad. And then on Saturday, I'll cook you a real Filipino dinner."

The promise of a future date seemed to cheer the pregnant woman. They walked to a convenience store and purchased bacon bits (Maribel's selection) and fragrant white rice. On the way home, Nicolette carried the groceries while Maribel waddled beside her, her hands cradling her belly.

"You were cheating on Peter," Maribel said, "and you left *him?*"

Nicolette nodded. It was a small lie. She switched the plastic bag to her other hand. For once she felt like the gatekeeper, that she had traded places with her ex-boyfriend and his excuses. In reality, Peter drank excessively and ran around with other girls, claiming to study late in the Ateneo library. She nudged George Ramos, Peter's solemn best friend, about her boyfriend's whereabouts whenever they made their rounds together at Makati Medical Center. But Nicolette couldn't admit to a married woman like Maribel that it had taken her four years to stop deceiving herself about a man.

Nicolette said, "I was talking to Peter and a group of our friends at The Giraffe—this nightclub where the up-and-coming bands play. One night Peter was drunk and George tried to quiet him down. But Peter continued heckling the band, throwing San Miguel bottles on stage, ordering all of the waiters around." She scratched the inside of her wrist. "So I left The Giraffe that night and went home with George. And when my visa was approved, I left them both."

"How did you end up in Boston?"

"I may have a nursing position at a school for deaf children."

"You don't have it yet?" Maribel asked.

"I have to master sign language first."

Maribel grabbed her lightly by the wrist. "Did Peter know that you were seeing George?"

They paused before a sycamore tree that had created a fault in the sidewalk with its thick, knotted roots. Nicolette set the plastic bags on the sidewalk, massaging the puffy welts where they had dug into her fingers. Above them the moon and stars were scattered like a rubber ball and jacks across the sky.

Maribel's lips were parted, waiting.

"If I told Peter I was cheating with his best friend, who knows what he would have done?" It was a bit melodramatic, but she felt encouraged and flattered by the pregnant woman's attention. Of course, Peter was the one who had left The Giraffe that night with one of *her* girlfriends, while she was in the bathroom fixing her long black hair. George Ramos had refused to leave with Peter, though, and waited for her outside the ladies' room. He was a shy, homely man that in her finickiness she had never considered dating.

*

Maribel called Nicolette the following afternoon at her temp job—word processing for a law firm with five names. Nicolette stared out her picture window at the round courthouse across the way, thinking it looked like a wedding cake with one slice removed.

"We're meeting one of Thomas's friends tonight," Maribel said. "I think you'd like him. Sammy's a musician."

"Is he Filipino?"

"Does it matter?"

Nicolette spun in her chair and watched the curly-haired man who shared her cubicle surf the Internet. It did matter. Nicolette thought Filipinos should date Filipinos, not Americans or blacks or *incheks*—Chinese. She'd never mentioned this to Maribel; the pregnant woman was too occupied with her baby and her own trivial problems. Besides, her husband, Thomas, was an American—a stocky, blonde-haired man who looked as if he'd stumbled into his life rather than earned it. When Maribel introduced him the previous evening over Cobb salads, he mumbled a few words about his practice and went to bed. Nicolette admired the way he moved in his grey sweats, and hated herself for noticing. Nothing made up for the fact that Thomas and Maribel's daughter would be only half-Filipino. Maribel, it seemed, had lost all sense of her culture. All that Nicolette sensed in the woman now speaking intimately to her on the other end of the telephone was a love for her husband, easy-to-prepare meals, and gossip about the other students in their weekly sign language class.

Nicolette's coworker smiled at her, revealing yellow teeth. She turned and faced the window.

"*Sige na*," she whispered into the telephone, though she wasn't interested in a blind date. At that moment it seemed more appealing than making another excuse to the yellow-teethed coworker, who asked her out for drinks every night.

*

Maribel leaned into Nicolette in the loud pool hall. "Doesn't he remind you of Franklin?"

Nicolette shrugged, blowing smoke in the opposite direction of Maribel. Thomas and his friend Sammy played billiards on a red felt table. Sammy moved stiffly, a human coatrack, in his ragged wool blazer and ill-fitting pants. Nicolette saw the resemblance to their teacher, the awkwardness and laconic air, but Sammy wore thicker spectacles. Nicolette imagined him the type to hound a student rather than nurture her, as Franklin did.

"Sammy's written an operetta," Maribel whispered. "Do you know any Filipinos who've done that?"

Nicolette sensed the woman's eagerness to please. Maribel had pulled her long hair through the opening in her baseball cap this evening, and Nicolette wanted to share a story about cutting her own long hair as a kind of statement, once she'd told Peter that she was leaving him (moving across the world away from him, actually, to a new life in Boston). How would the attractive woman react? She seemed to place a great emphasis on appearance. Even the bulky Patriots jacket she wore tonight must have been carefully chosen because it belonged to her husband. Nicolette hated women who clung to their lovers, in conversation or otherwise.

She stubbed her cigarette in a paper ashtray. Thomas winked at them, grinding his hips to the eighties music that filled the lofty warehouse. Sammy leaned against the wall, crumpled almost, awaiting his turn. He had greeted Nicolette brusquely when she arrived and then returned to his game with Thomas. To Nicolette the room felt heavy with noise: electronic video games, billiard balls ricocheting off bumpers, and the loud, drunken voices of three women at the table next to them. Why had she exchanged a night alone for this crowded hall?

She turned to Maribel and asked, "What will you name the baby?"

Maribel smiled. "Is this part of the interview?" She reached for her virgin daiquiri and sipped from the straw. Her cheeks looked shiny tonight. "Thomas wants to name her *Alison,* but I think *Missy* is nice." Did she just bat her eyelids? An image came to Nicolette of the tourists in Baclaran holding a commode in the air and proclaiming, "Look, honey, isn't it cute!"

While Maribel prattled about baby names, Nicolette began to search her purse for more cigarettes. Sometimes she wished she weren't so hard.

"Those are interesting names," she said, placing a package of facial tissues and a cell phone on the table. She avoided making eye contact with Maribel. "You know, Peter and I used to talk about baby names. His favorite was *Manolo.* Mine was very close to your name, Maribel—I liked *Michelle."* Of course, she had never talked to Peter about children. They barely agreed on a restaurant for their midday merienda. She was at the bottom of her purse and came up with one last cigarette. Why so many lies? She tried to relate it to smoking: more hazardous to herself than those around her. Nothing was that bad in moderation.

Maribel had grown quiet. Nicolette lit her cigarette, watching the other woman in thought, enjoying her soft profile. Maribel's face was not as plump as she had imagined, less round even than the women in her family, and her cheeks did not shine as she first thought. They listened to the young women at the next table share confidences about a recalcitrant lover. The trio of voices reminded Nicolette of pigeons cooing on the Esplanade.

After a while, Maribel spoke.

"Do you want to know what I'm afraid of?"

Nicolette guessed childbirth.

Maribel dotted her lips with her napkin. The intensity of Maribel's gaze shamed her. "I'm afraid that Thomas will leave me. That this baby, even though it's the only thing keeping us together, that it'll make him hate me even more."

She paused, sipped her frothy drink. She watched the men at the large pool table. Nicolette sensed it was her turn to ask Maribel questions, to listen to the woman's afflictions, to soothe her disquiet. What a silly game it was, becoming friends. How did Thomas and Sammy manage? In Manila, at the hospital where she had worked with shy George Ramos, she learned to separate friendship from work. *There are many kinds of caretaking,* she told Menchie. *Nursing is the only paying one.* Now she watched as Thomas, in his familiar gray sweatpants, stretched against the edge of the table. He aimed his cue stick at a lonely ball in the corner.

Nicolette said nothing to Maribel.

Maribel's needs went beyond a patient's. She wanted to pose Nicolette on a polished mantel, beside Sammy and the rest of her American friends, coupled people expecting marriage, children, and quaint decorative commodes. Nicolette wanted none of it. Maribel's friends read *Cosmo* and talked in slang, made the boozy sounds that filled this crowded pool hall. When she looked around the room, Nicolette was shocked to find Sammy planted in a high-backed chair facing her, staring over his pint of dark beer.

There was only one thing that could distract her from her goals, and it was something that this Sammy—brooding in his beer like an artist—could not provide.

*

On Saturday evening, Nicolette carried ten bulbs of garlic, a bottle of Kikkoman soy sauce, and one pound of pork hocks to Maribel's condominium to cook dinner. She also remembered a small microcassette recorder borrowed from the law firm. Tonight, she decided, they would finish the interview so that she could practice her biography before class. It would be the last night of her odd friendship with Maribel.

In the living room, Nicolette allowed Thomas to take her coat. "Maribel's creating a mess in the kitchen," he joked. From the sofa, Sammy stood (Nicolette had forgotten he was so tall) and kissed her awkwardly on the cheek. She blushed, surprised by the kiss; he seemed more outgoing than the previous night, when he and Thomas had played pool and ignored the women. "It's great to see you," he said, smiling. He had striking blue eyes. Distracted, she returned his greeting and hurried into the kitchen.

Maribel greeted her with a kiss as well. She took the groceries from Nicolette and placed them on the counter.

Red lettuce leaves were drying on paper towels beside the microwave. "I told Thomas and Sammy it's Filipino night, so they're prepared," Maribel said, winking. Nicolette wondered if Maribel was always this happy. She remembered Maribel's disclosure last night in the pool hall. Thomas was so typical, so unremarkably male: why didn't she leave *him*? "It's easier with Sammy," Maribel continued, "he practically lives for ethnic food. Once he brought us to an Ethiopian restaurant, and we had to mop up this soupy thing with our hands! He's up for anything."

The pregnant woman scurried around her kitchen, and Nicolette sensed that she had prepared plenty of small talk for this evening. Sammy entered and stood in the doorjamb next to Nicolette.

Maribel said, "Sammy just got a promotion at the New England Conservatory."

"It's not a big deal," he said. "Now I'm a hired hand with benefits." He placed his hand gently on Nicolette's back. It was something Peter never would have done. "It's more babysitting than anything."

Sammy talked about the difficulty of training his students for careers in music. Not everyone was going to play in a major symphony orchestra. As he spoke, Nicolette let his hand remain on her lower back, meeting his eyes at times. She liked the neat part in his hair, the way it waved up and then fell to one side. Before she could stop herself, she was smiling, a wide, silly grin that instantly embarrassed her. They stared at each other a moment before Nicolette shook free.

"I should prepare the adobo." Maribel made room beside her on the counter.

"I'm sorry I was so aloof last night," Sammy said to Nicolette and Maribel. "Three of my students skipped their lessons, and I spent all afternoon waiting for them in a damp room."

Nicolette wondered if Maribel had prepped him about the right things to say. In a long drawer, she found a tablespoon and used its curved back to break the husk of a garlic clove. When she looked up, Sammy was still idling in the doorway. He held one hand to the back of his neck, unsure of himself. Nicolette said, "Here we are again, Maribel—the women doing all the work."

"I'll help!" Sammy said. "Tell me what to do."

She put him to work chopping the garlic (*not too fine*, Nicolette said, *it reduces all the flavor*), and the three of them shared a bottle of merlot while the adobo simmered on the stove. Eventually Maribel went to the dining room to help Thomas set the table. The sky had grown dark outside the tall kitchen window, and Sammy apologized to Nicolette again for his sulkiness in the pool hall. His moods came and went, he said, in direct proportion to the number of students he was assigned each semester.

"Perhaps you should find another job," Nicolette said.

"There isn't much work for a classical pianist. Paying jobs, at least."

"And when do you compose your music?"

"Probably when you're sound asleep." He set his wine glass on the counter and moved next to her. She could smell the wine on his breath. "Sometimes I write at night, but my mind's always racing. So I wake up before dawn. I try to find a quiet time." This reminded her of reading her novels in the morning, when her neighborhood was silent except for the T outside her window, steeling on its tracks.

Sammy cleared his throat. "Can I ask you a personal question, Nicolette?"

She stirred the pot simmering on the stove. The cubes of pork had begun to separate from its bones.

Her back to him, she shrugged.

"Are you seeing anyone?"

What could she say? That she wasn't interested in dating? Or that she wasn't interested in Americans? "I have a boyfriend," she replied. She leaned down to the adobo and tasted the vinegary broth.

"Oh," Sammy said, staring into his wine glass. "That's too bad." He drank the rest of his wine. "If you *were* available, I'd ask you on a proper date."

Nicolette replaced the round lid on the pot. When she looked up she saw Maribel over Sammy's shoulder, listening to them in the doorway. How much had she heard? Maribel glared, and Nicolette knew that she had seen through the lie.

"*Kain na,*" Maribel quipped. She strode to the counter and spooned rice from the steaming rice cooker into a bowl. She avoided eye contact with Nicolette. "My mom taught me the meaning of *kain na,* Sammy. It means, 'Let's eat.'"

*

Following Maribel's dinner party, Nicolette expected other invitations to follow. She would be aloof toward Maribel, indifferent when Sammy called. Neither phoned. The following week, October's last, the two women stood in front of the sign language class to share their biographies. They hadn't discussed what they were going to say. Nicolette had decided that her half of the assignment would be succinct and professional, relating only the facts. She hoped Maribel would do the same.

Nicolette held out her right hand and spelled Maribel's name. "Worcester, Born—She," she signed, "Wellesley, School—Went. Married. Pregnant."

She continued: "First Child—Girl—One Month."

"Point your fingers out, lady," a man with a husky voice shouted from the back of the tiled room.

Nicolette sighed, spelling Thomas's name and explaining that he was the husband. She turned to Maribel. The pregnant woman half-sat on the table with her arms crossed. There was a small wooden lectern between them, Franklin's bag of pistachios, and a smattering of colored pencils. Maribel picked up a blue pencil and rolled it between her thumb and fingers, pretending to ignore her partner. If Maribel wouldn't even look at her, what more was there to say?

Nicolette made the sign for *thank you* and the class applauded. Franklin removed his wire spectacles, nodding so that Nicolette saw him. And though she knew she wasn't being supportive, Nicolette moved to an empty desk in the front row and faced Maribel. She looked at the clock. There was ten minutes left of class.

Maribel straightened, and smoothed her white maternity dress over her stomach. She raised her left hand and spelled Nicolette's name. Then, switching to her right hand, slowly—as if she'd just memorized the alphabet—she spelled, "P-H-I-L-I-P-P-I-N-E-S." Nicolette smirked. The other woman's range was limited.

"Tough, She."

Weak, She, Nicolette thought.

"Job: Nurse People."

Job: Bother People.

Maribel glanced at Nicolette, seated in the front row. She seemed to understand the look of annoyance on Nicolette's face but chose to face her classmates. "Friend, She. Mine," the pregnant woman signed, pointing at herself.

Then she smiled, adding: "Tough Cookie."

The class laughed, and Maribel took the seat she always did, behind Nicolette. The pregnant woman had to be mocking her. To the rest of the class, they appeared to be friends.

Franklin praised the couple and inserted a videotape in the VCR. A deaf actor and actress communicated with each other, their words translated in red letters at the bottom of the frame. Nicolette sighed; she could feel Maribel grinning in the seat behind her. In her mind the class was over and she had returned to her studio apartment alone.

Wrestlers

Thomas McCusker writhed on a red plastic mat with his young brother-in-law, their necks wet and legs intertwined. Thomas, a hulking man, would have weighed in at 225 pounds if he were still competing. Noel Borgos, his brother-in-law and an alternate on the team, ate once a day and fell into a 112 or 119 class.

The boy lunged at him and wrapped his arms tightly around Thomas's chest, his head burrowing into Thomas's stomach. The group of high school boys encircling them moved closer.

Kneeling, Thomas countered at an easy pace, reaching over Noel's backside and locking his arms around his flat stomach. As the coach of the team (he was only twenty-seven, ten years older than the boys), he wanted to teach them control. He gripped the boy snugly, not as he would an opponent of his own heft or experience, but with a sure hold, pleased by Noel's aggression and sense of resolve. But after ten seconds of squirreling, he felt the boy's arms grow slack.

He loosened his grip on Noel.

Noel seized the opportunity, breaking away and wrenching Thomas's left arm behind his back. With a locked elbow, he forced Thomas to the floor, head to the mat, the tightly stretched plastic burning his cheek. Thomas lay still, balanced perilously on one hip. He could easily wriggle free. But if the boy was less powerful than his opponent, at a disadvantage in size or strength, he'd teach him to maximize opportunity—to recognize a weak wrist or sloppy traction—when it presented itself in a six-minute match.

"Watch my eyes, Noel!"

Thomas counted silently from one to ten, staring at the faint brown eyes an inch or two from his own. Noel's attention was somewhere beyond the door that had been propped open to ventilate the winter-warm room. He recognized in Noel's thin face the startled but unmoving expression of a raccoon he'd surprised once, when his wife had nagged him late one night to throw out the garbage.

Thomas abandoned his countdown and began to lift himself from the mat with one hand. "OK, Noel," he said, "Let go."

Dazed, the boy released his wrist. They separated and Noel leaned back, elbows on the mat, pushing air through his lips like a broken car muffler.

Thomas stood and pressed his palms into his thighs for support. The boys hunched in a circle around them applauded.

"When you've got the advantage, Noel, take it. Control is everything."

*

From his office in the rear of the locker room, Thomas had a view of the enormous dressing area that fronted the showers. On Saturday mornings his pockmarked teenagers had the run of the place, their rowdy hollers rising with the steam and the stiff odor of sweat. Through his window, he watched Marcus Henley—a fourth-year wrestler and the team captain—approach his office, before turning to shout over his shoulder at his teammates. *Hey, queers, what are you looking at?* he said, grinning. He posed in front of Thomas's window and toweled his wide V-shaped back. *Get a load of this ass,* he continued, teasing the other wrestlers still lingering in the showers. When Thomas caught his eye, Marcus smiled: wide and gap-toothed, a child's.

Noel put his hand on Marcus's back to pass behind him. Thomas glanced down at his desk, pretending to write in his yellow pad.

"Let's go," Noel said, entering the office. "Marcus said he'd lock up."

The boy rapped his knuckles on the metal desk. His wild black hair was uncombed, and one ear was pierced with a gold hoop near the top. Noel was seventeen years old, scrawnier than the other boys, and he hadn't yet learned to drive. He was more helpless than anyone Thomas had ever met. When he married Maribel, he hadn't realized how clingy her brother would become. Now he watched the boy collapse in a folding chair across from him, feeling guilty for harping on Noel's helplessness. It wasn't the boy's fault he'd grown up in a house of overbearing women. He was the exact opposite of Marcus.

"Don't they have Driver's Ed in your country?" Thomas said without looking up. He forced the image of Marcus's body, wet and naked, from his mind.

Noel laughed. "You mean the United States?"

"I mean the land where your people come from. You know—your family, my wife."

"You make funny, Thomas! I tell Maribel you make big funny." He shook his head and unwrapped the metallic foil on a stick of gum.

Thomas put his notes from the morning practice in his gym bag. He was pleased his boys had wrestled well. Regionals were the next morning—a measure of his coaching ability—and he had no doubt Marcus Henley would perform. Noel was another case. Winning, of course, wasn't the point (*Just give it your hardest,* he had coached Marcus to tell the team), but for Noel's sake he hoped the boy wouldn't get pinned. He liked Noel enough; he didn't do drugs or raise hell for his mother, Teresa, a pediatric nurse at Brigham and Women's Hospital. During holidays at the Borgos house, Thomas often hid in the boy's room, playing video games and drinking beer from a bottle.

He looked through the black-lined window and saw Marcus prop one foot on a bench, drying his legs. Marcus shrugged when he caught Thomas's eye, a sort of "What can you do?" on his face, and walked away, his thin, pilling towel hanging over his shoulder like a sash. He strutted past the other boys in the showers, his chest inflated as if he'd bought a new hat. Then he turned a corner of wire lockers and disappeared.

Thomas stood and lowered the aluminum blinds. When he turned, he noticed Noel had been watching, too. The boy was cockier, more ready to gambit than anyone Thomas had ever met. The boy cleared his throat and sat up straight in the folding chair.

"There's just something about all that grabbing, Thomas. You know, other guys touching you everywhere? Their arms and legs all sweaty and stuff." He paused. How he liked to push Thomas's buttons! "You've been wrestling a long time, right? You ever get excited?"

Thomas capped his ballpoint pen. "I'm not queer, Noel. What do you think this sport's about?" He zipped his black bag. Noel and Maribel were always playing stupid games. Last Christmas, Maribel had given Noel a small purple gift book called *One Thousand and One Questions If You Were God.* She and her little brother were inseparable. When he was in their company—as he often was during this time, Noel's last year in high school—he found himself nodding, smiling, and tuning out.

"But don't you think all that rolling around could, like, get somebody excited?" Noel reached to his ear and caressed his gold hoop. "I could've sworn I saw Marcus with a little bulge today."

Thomas wanted to complete his errands and drop Noel at his mother's house before the Patriots played Pittsburgh. It was already past noon, and he knew that if he didn't hurry he'd miss the kickoff. Worse, his unhappy wife would explode at him for his tardiness.

"Grab your stuff, Noel," he said. "We're late."

In the school parking lot he started his Jeep, then remembered his sunglasses inside the locker room. *An accessory,* he said to Noel, *but necessary*—the bright snow, the icy roads glistening in the afternoon sun. He left the motor running and hustled back inside, past the long rows of metal lockers, into the wide-open dressing area, where he feigned disinterest in the whooping calls of his boys.

*

Thomas looked up from the saucepan. Maribel was staring at him, waiting for his answer.

"Deaf—whatever."

"Really? I'd say blind."

He shrugged, sipping his bottle of beer. He wasn't interested in playing her games, anyway. She had entered the kitchen and barraged him with philosophical questions: *Do you think it's more important to love or be loved? If you had to choose, which would you be: deaf or blind?* They were meant to tease out his values but he found them crass. He wanted to finish cooking their pasta so he could watch the game on their large-screen TV. The microwave beeped five times, and Maribel opened the door and removed a small green bowl.

She poured the white-streaked butter in the bowl over her popcorn, analyzing his answer. Thomas stirred the pasta, thinking of Marcus Henley in the locker room, drying his V-shaped back.

Maribel leaned against the counter and tossed a kernel of popcorn in the air. Her dark waist-length hair fell over her shoulders, and her compact frame looked strange with the round belly that protruded from her middle. At times like this, he felt as if he were in a movie where a character woke up in someone else's dream. Did everyone have that feeling? Lately, when he thought of the baby, his work, and his life with Maribel, he realized that, barely even thirty, he was living the life of his father, an aging company man in New Jersey. Maribel smiled at him. She then missed several kernels in a row.

His wife bent at the knees and reached to the linoleum, sweeping the kernels into her hands and eating them. She moved to the tall kitchen window. Her pear-shaped profile was backlit by a belt of late afternoon sun. With one hand she parted the lace curtains. With the other, she rubbed her stomach. Dr. Cureg had told them the baby was a girl. Maribel was due in less than a month; without consulting her husband, she had asked Noel to be the godfather.

"I showed your brother a Crab Ride this morning," he said, "but it's like talking to a stop sign. He can't focus."

"I think he's just preoccupied."

"You and your mom baby him too much." Thomas removed his thick Patriots sweatshirt and then tucked his white T-shirt into his jeans. He wondered if Maribel understood what he did: that her brother was queer. It seemed obvious in the way he talked, the way he watched the other wrestlers during practice and, afterward, in the locker room when they showered and dressed. "Noel's a man, for Christ's sake. You should treat him like one."

Maribel was unmoved. She shook salt on her popcorn and then wiped her hands on her batik dress. "Have you ever thought he's struggling with something other than wrestling? Girls, maybe? Getting into a good school?"

"Have you ever thought you might be coddling him?"

"Quit changing the subject, Thomas."

The water in the shallow saucepan bubbled over the edge and sizzled on the electric coil. Thomas turned the heat to low and stirred the foamy water. The Borgos family was crazy. "Hand me that sieve, Maribel."

She reached into the sink and pointed at him with the sieve. "Do you think this baby's ever going to come out?"

Thomas stirred the pasta, listening to her complain about her sore feet and back. He lifted the saucepan from the burner while she continued to ramble, changing the subject to Noel's duties as godparent. She was more talkative than usual and he thought of how little she had changed from the first time they had met, when they lived in the same building at the foot of Beacon Hill. One night after his run along Memorial Drive, over the MIT bridge and along the landscaped esplanade, the elevator doors of his building opened and Maribel stood inside. "You look like hell," she said then, and he had; but most people, especially strangers, would have kept this to themselves.

Thomas poured the steaming water, the long green strands of pasta, and the dollop of olive oil into the sieve. Water dribbled from the bottom in the sink.

Maribel pulled a strand of pasta from the side of the pan and ate it. "Do you think Noel's gay and just scared to tell me?" She looked at Thomas. "I mean it'd be weird, but he's my brother."

*

Maybe it was his wife and Noel's babble about sexuality: Thomas wanted to have sex. From the kitchen, she told him to go to the bathroom and jerk off. Her tone wasn't rude but in the manner of a nurse who tells her patient to pee in a cup.

"Besides," she called out, "my mother told me sex will traumatize the baby."

How did her family creep into every conversation? Thomas closed the bathroom door and ran a bath.

He undressed quickly, throwing his denim jeans and T-shirt in a pile on the floor. He reminded himself that his mood-swinging wife was due soon, that her life was consumed by the baby writhing in her stomach. He closed the faucet and lowered himself into the hot water, his toes and the backs of his knees absorbing the heat. His eyes closed, he reached under the water and began to touch himself.

The phone rang in the hallway. He listened to Maribel's stale voice.

"It's no big deal, Noel. I'll ask him when he unlocks the door."

Thomas gave up and bent his knees, sliding his body down the length of the smooth porcelain tub. Regionals in the morning, his ravenous wife, her queer younger brother. An overdue haircut, his baby, Marcus Henley—*no, not Marcus Henley*—their sure, immutable hold. Just that morning, driving Noel home, he'd lectured the boy on decisiveness, on thinking of his future as an opponent he should wrestle into a headlock.

He opened his eyes, leaning his head on the lip of the tub. Maribel hated it, but everything *did* come back to wrestling. Either you took hold of your life or you got pinned.

*

Thomas drove through Central Square without slowing for pedestrians and down the busy length of Mass Ave. It was nearly midnight, and he and Noel had spent the evening in a cinder-block auditorium, listening to an admissions counselor dole out advice to a group of bored students and parents.

"That admissions guy needs a life," Noel said.

Thomas shrugged. The evening was shot, as far as he was concerned, but why encourage Noel's complaints? He watched the boy pull down the visor and smooth his messy black hair in the mirror. The bus he'd arranged to take his wrestlers to regionals in the morning would leave in a few hours. "You better just crash on our couch," Thomas said. "It'll be easier than picking you up in the morning."

Noel groaned. Earlier that evening, in the crowded auditorium, Thomas had noticed the boy's restlessness, the way he tapped his feet on the floor and fidgeted in his seat. Now, as they drove to the middle of the concrete bridge that crossed the Charles River, Thomas wondered if Noel was worried about the tournament. Traffic on the bridge crept slowly; he could have walked more quickly than they were moving. Finally, he stopped his Jeep and put it into park. It was odd; jogging on this bridge after work, he'd weaved between pedestrians on the sidewalk and never noticed the car traffic. Now horns beeped behind them. Thomas drummed his fingers on the dashboard, and his eyes followed the parallel red lines formed by the taillights ahead of them. They could have been sitting on a runway at Logan rather than the MIT bridge.

A police officer in a white helmet approached. "It'll be a while, guys. A truck driver crashed into some college kids."

Thomas rolled up his window and looked at Noel, who shrugged. The cell phone in his back pocket pressed into his rear. He removed it, tossing it on the seat. The honking behind them faded.

Thomas leaned against his door and stared at the mound of short, stunted buildings across the river on Beacon Hill. The far-off mound reminded him of Maribel's stomach as she lay on her back in bed. He reached for his keys and killed the engine.

"I can't wait for her to give birth," he mumbled, not realizing he'd spoken aloud until Noel asked him to repeat himself.

"I was thinking about Maribel. How miserable she is. *I'd* get pregnant if it meant one less day of her moods."

"You didn't spend twelve years living with her."

Thomas laughed, wiping the fogged glass with his fist. "No, I married her instead."

Noel fidgeted in his seat. Traffic was silent in both lanes. After a while, the boy spoke.

"Thomas? What would you say if—" he fidgeted with the string of his hooded sweatshirt, chewing on the plastic ends. They made a crunching sound between his teeth. "It's just, I guess—what would you think if I was dating another guy?"

"Dating?"

"You know, seeing this person."

Thomas shifted uncomfortably. "Sure, Noel—you've gotta have a buddy to run around with."

"I'm sleeping with this buddy."

"Jesus, Noel! No descriptions necessary."

The boy laughed self-consciously. Thomas stared ahead, through his windshield, holding the steering wheel as if the Jeep might move on its own accord. He read the raised white numbers and letters of a blue license plate without comprehending them. What was Noel talking about? He wished the boy was running up his phone bill or talking with his wife at home, instead of sitting in his car. She would know how to talk him out of this crazy idea.

The boy turned his back to him, facing the passenger door. Thomas closed his eyes and leaned back against the headrest. In his mind he saw Maribel atop their comforter, pointing the remote control in the air with one hand, slowly rubbing her belly with the other.

Suddenly he felt a gentle tugging at his waist. He opened his eyes. Noel was bent in his lap, undoing his leather belt. What was he doing? Thomas had never thought of him like this before. There had been one time, as a sophomore at Rutgers, when he and his friend Donnie went back to his place after a long night of drinking. Donnie had a joint in his desk, and they smoked it before passing out in bed. Thomas remembered waking in the middle of the night, his stomach rumbling from the beer and the pot, and Donnie jerking him off beneath the sheets. He kept his eyes closed as Donnie continued and he quickly came. When he opened his eyes, the sheets glowed in the hard light from the streetlamps, their bodies curled into a three-dimensional map of some mountain range. He rolled away from Donnie, onto his stomach, and sighed into the pillow, unsure of what to think or say. The pillow smelled of Donnie's cologne. Soon Thomas crept out of the bed and across the grassy quad to his own apartment, his underwear stuffed in a jeans pocket. Neither he nor Donnie had ever mentioned it.

In the front seat of his Jeep, Thomas was hard. Slowly, he took Noel's wrist and coaxed it into his briefs. The boy reached under the elastic band, grabbed his penis, and began rubbing it. Thomas moaned.

A horn blared from the car behind them and he pushed the boy away. Noel sat upright, his cheeks flushed, saying, "I didn't mean to gross you out, Thomas. I mean, you seemed like you wanted to—"

"Just shut up for a second."

Thomas fumbled with his underwear and zipped the fly of his worn jeans. What the hell were they doing? He wanted it to be the boy's fault. He buckled his belt and straightened it across his waist. The runway lights in front of them blinked and then disappeared.

He started the engine and drove toward the shore. Glancing down at the seat, he saw the boy's fingers outspread, as if they had small suction cups. The skin around the knuckles was knicked—from practice, he assumed. Or could they be from the "friend" he was sleeping with? Traffic flowed steadily. What had just happened, what had *almost* happened in the front seat, Thomas decided, was a fluke. It was late; they were tired and sleepy. At the intersection of Beacon Street and Mass Ave he stepped hard on the brakes. In the passenger seat Noel balked, reaching for his gray hood and pulling it over his head. Would he tell Maribel?

The white-helmeted officer in the middle of the intersection blew his whistle and then pointed at him, motioning for him to cross the red light.

Thomas stepped on the accelerator.

"You're not gay," he said to the boy, who was slumped in the seat with his arms crossed. Noel didn't respond. Thomas steered into the opposite lane, past the police officer, and sped home to his wife.

*

One hundred and thirty-two boys in shiny unitards and rustling warm-up outfits gathered in the middle school gymnasium. The crackly voice of an announcer echoed through the vaulted room. From a stage recessed in the northern wall, Thomas watched his squad of teenagers across the gymnasium. Marcus was entertaining them with a story, his exaggerated motions like a street juggler. Noel sat on the edge of the mat apart from them talking with Chad Kline, a redheaded sophomore whose family had just moved here from the West Coast.

The announcer, in matching gray sweatshirt and pants, quietly told the coaches the final matchups. Thomas watched the man's gestures, remembering the previous evening and the image of Noel in his lap. Why was the boy so bold? Did he sense something queer about *him*? They had driven to the condo in silence, Maribel asleep when they arrived. In the morning she'd mumbled a listless "good luck" before rolling to the side of the bed against the wall.

Thomas stepped down from the stage and went to his boys. He tapped Noel's shoulder and motioned for the boy to follow him to a small alcove between the bleachers and a painted wall. He didn't want to focus on what happened last night. Instead, he wanted to psych the boy up to wrestle: Noel's opponent was a clumsy wrestler from a wealthy Boston suburb. He knew if Noel wrestled well, the team might still place.

Noel bounced in his tightly laced shoes.

"This guy's an amateur, Noel. You've got a real chance."

He continued bouncing. Thomas grasped his shoulders and forced him to stop. Noel stared at him with disinterest, then at the ground.

"What happened last night?" Noel asked. He traced a groove between cinder blocks with his finger. "I mean, I know I shouldn't have—"

"Noel, listen to me. You can win this match, easy. In fact, you can pull it off for the entire squad." He checked his watch while Noel slumped against the wall. There wasn't time for the boy's stupid games; his match started in a few minutes.

"Is that all that's important to you? A bunch of guys wrestling on a mat?" He was breathing hard and had unsnapped his head-gear. The chinstrap dangled at his cheek. Thomas wanted to shake him by the shoulders, anything, to quit his babbling and make him focus on the matter at hand.

The boy moved close to him. Thomas could feel his fast breathing on his face.

"Winning doesn't prove anything," he said, staring into his eyes. "Everybody on the team still thinks you're gay."

*

Later the team loaded their gear in the first few seats of the school bus. They hadn't placed, but his boys seemed spirited nonetheless. From the sidewalk Thomas watched them mount the stairs, Noel and Chad Kline in front. They sat together in a padded seat near the middle of the bus.

Thomas felt his cell phone vibrate and removed it from his back pocket. It was Maribel.

She talked as if they were standing in the same room. Thomas could see Noel leaning into his friend to share a secret. He stood on the empty sidewalk, listening patiently to his wife, and when she asked recounted the day's defeats.

The Foley Artist

Berong lived in a two-bedroom apartment above a retail store that sold pornography in West Hollywood. Because he had spent his life adding sound effects to motion pictures—cushioned footfalls on parquet floors, any number of seagulls and crashing waves on boardwalks, the turbulent construction noises and traffic of a midtown avenue in Manhattan—he cared little for the winsome tones of the human voice. Dialogue would never hold as much resonance as, say, five carefully placed elevator pings. At one time in his life, when he was younger than his seventy-nine years, he'd obliged in small talk, engaging a chatty girl he soon married. Their daughter, Maribel, was born in 1969. But impatient with his wife's pleading and the selfless demands of domesticity, Berong soon walked out. One night, moved by drink and an unfamiliar longing for others, he telephoned his wife in Boston and asked to speak with their child. She informed him the teenager had run off with a long-haired musician, then hung up. Berong sat alone in a dingy Chinatown hotel, the receiver limp in his hand, watching a hairy centipede scuttle around the one-toed sandal on his left foot. Instead of the harsh bleating of the telephone, he wanted to Foley a more evocative click.

Though he had lived there for twenty-two years, he had never set foot in the succession of stores below his apartment. A medical supply store when he moved in, the space had gone through multiple reincarnations, at various times a lunch counter, a busy pawn shop, and now a store that sold pornography. When he was working, Berong was infrequently in the apartment, traveling from editing suites to home to crowded docks with his NAGRA to record the lazy hum of the crowd or the blare of a barge horn as it pulled away from shore. At times, moved by sudden impulse, he would open his eyes, turn off his NAGRA, and watch the crowd drift and bottleneck. Once he retired, his habits were inverted and he spent most of his days in his apartment. He sold his car and rode the bus to the grocery store, the public library, and a well-stocked video store near Paramount owned by a Filipino.

Berong's parents were dead, his two older brothers were in a faraway province of Ilocos, and the person most familiar with him was Manolo, the Filipino video store owner, formerly a property master who had worked with Berong on a small-budget film called *Night of Desire*. A friendly but not gregarious person, Manolo called Berong *padre* and often invited him to his home to celebrate holidays and his children's birthdays. But because Berong never accepted, Manolo, deciding the elderly Filipino a snob, stopped extending the invitations.

One wet afternoon Manolo and Berong quarreled over the older man's account, Manolo accusing Berong of unpaid fees.

Certain he was in the right, Berong walked out of the video store and selected a Blockbuster in West Hollywood, resolving never to call on Manolo again.

Several days passed. Berong watched Telemundo and Technicolor westerns with the volume turned off and the loud engine of a bus or the heavy bass rhythm of a car speaker drifting through his window. One morning he scanned his large video library, selected a film in Italian, and inserted the tape into his VCR. The .VCR would not play. Berong unplugged the machine and tinkered with it. Unwilling to consult Manolo at the video shop, he hobbled downstairs to the pornography store in hopes of purchasing a new VCR.

*

Inside the store, a stocky red-haired boy who seemed more like a wrestler than a clerk hummed to himself behind a high counter. His plain nametag read *CHAD*. The boy glanced at the older man, then returned to his adult magazine. Berong asked about purchasing a VCR. The clerk laughed.

"Can you please order me one?" Berong asked.

"Try a department store," Chad replied. Two middle-aged men in cut-off jeans whispered behind Berong. Chad repeated to Berong that he didn't have what he wanted.

"You should care about your work," said Berong, and left.

Berong went upstairs and sat in a sagging armchair. Air from the cushions escaped slowly. Berong imagined instead the crisp springs of a metal bed. He stood and went into the kitchen. He could ride a bus to the shapeless shopping mall near the Pacific Coast Highway, but discerning the simplest route seemed exhausting. He opened a drawer near the sink and found a business card with Manolo's phone number. He went to his phone in the living room, lifted the receiver. Then replaced it again. He would not call the disrespectful young man.

The next morning Berong again entered the windowless shop. He stepped to the counter and asked Chad to order his VCR.

Chad slurped noodles with chopsticks from a pint-sized container. "It's not going to happen," the red-haired boy said.

"Please, I live upstairs."

"What do you want from me?" Chad asked. "Find someone else to harass."

Berong said, "I'm asking so little."

Chad hooked a finger into his ear and dug around. He sighed. In the concave mirror hung in one corner, he glanced at a trio of young men touching the CD-ROMs. One CD clattered out of its package to the ground. Berong stared at him.

"Here's a coupon for a free rental. Just go."

Berong watched the clerk slide the yellow coupon across the counter. He remained standing in place. The dollar-sized coupon was neither the video player he desired nor a suitable replacement. For a second he wondered if the sound of the paper sliding across the counter could be mimicked with sand-paper on a hollow plywood door. It was habit, the residue of his lifework. Most of everyday life could be replaced with some-thing more evocative.

Berong stared at Chad's gaunt eyes above him, the young man's exasperation as obvious as the resolve he now felt. He took the yellow coupon, placed it in his shirt pocket, and sat on the sticky tile floor. Puzzled, Chad stood and peered over the edge of the tall counter.

The clerk pleaded with Berong for several minutes but the old man would not move. His back was straight and his eyes were closed as if he were meditating. Chad reached below the counter, placed a black telephone on top, and phoned the West Hollywood police. To Berong, the dialing sounded like the keys of a synthesizer being played. Within the hour two officers, their blue metal sunglasses perched like headbands, arrived. One officer spoke with Chad and the younger, more rotund one crouched and murmured to Berong. The old man sat with his eyes closed and said nothing. Finally, they lifted Berong, legs crossed like a pretzel, by his elbows and carried him from the store. They placed him on a vacant bus stop bench. Chad tended to the remaining customers and then followed Berong and the police officers outside.

Staring at the vacant lot across the street, Berong would not tell the officers where he lived. Chad, too, listened but did not speak.

When the officers stepped to their patrol car to confer, Chad bolted the shop and climbed the creaky stairs to Berong's apartment. The door was unlocked. On a table beside the telephone, Chad saw Manolo's card. He called the video store owner and explained the situation. Within the hour, Manolo parked his SUV in front of the bus stop. The officers left Berong in the younger man's care.

"Let's go upstairs, padre," said Manolo. A fly buzzed around Berong's collar.

"Maybe somebody died," said Chad, crouching in front of Berong, who was still seated on the bench.

Berong stared past the littered, six-lane boulevard. Behind a wire fence, he saw the skeleton of a school bus, sickly trees, and weeds sprouting from cracks in the pavement. He heard the rustle of palm trees in the provinces of his youth.

"I'll help you, Berong," Manolo said.

Berong saw a small bird hop across the roof of the bus. I'll help you, he thought to himself, flinching, for he had always considered himself an independent man. This phrase he associated with his wife, her meek voice repeating it time and again before he left. *I'll help you, padre,* he heard once more, and it seemed the most pathetic sound a voice could utter. Help, he whispered, watching the small bird jump down and hop across the weeds.

A Visit to California

We are leaving the steep cliff of California, embraced by the arm of a mountain, and the air is stale compared to the salty winds from the Pacific. Outside my window, a group of palm trees stands guard along the highway. Their formation reminds me of the palm trees lining the road from Manila to Visayas, their trunks thin and delicate, their palms outstretched like lovers.

The ride has been long, almost six days, and on the last leg, our bus driver—his name is Mazi—Mazi stopped our bus in Las Vegas, where I slept in an air-conditioned room with red velvet walls. Now I sit directly behind Mazi in his driver's seat. "Thank goodness for Vegas," I tell him. Our bus is winding into a deep valley and there is a toll booth ahead. "I don't want to surprise Noel with bags under my eyes!"

Mazi smiles up at me, lifting his single dark brow in the mirror. He cautiously steers our bus into an outside lane. The covered plaza ahead looks like my new dentures, with lines of automobiles like dental floss.

I remove a banana from the large hand-carried *bayong* at my feet and unpeel it. A compact automobile to my left is full of young people. They are loud and merry, with assorted limbs hanging outside of the car. An arm here, a bare foot there. They're laughing to rock and roll music, which reaches my ears through Mazi's open window, and I wonder: Could my Noel know them? I have not seen him in two full years. I hope he has made friends with other Filipinos.

At the beginning of his senior year, he called home from Stanford. I could hear the shouting of his friends and a stereo in the background, though I did not understand how his music was enjoyable when I could not make out the words. "It took forever to get Clea's couch in the door," he said in a booming voice. Someone in his dormitory room was also talking to him, and he spoke with me and this person at the same time. "You should see it here, Mom," he said, and as always, there was a polite distance in his voice. If he wants me to visit, then why has he never invited me? My next-door neighbor, Francine, was seated on a tall stool in my kitchen; I held the telephone a few inches from my ear while Noel continued to brag. When Francine looked up, I pointed at the loud noises coming from the receiver and she laughed. Then she returned to an old album I had found with photos of that awful football-helmet hairdo she used to wear in the seventies. Francine is a good friend; she baked cashew muffins for my family when we moved to Cambridge.

"I'm still here, Noel. Your sofa did not fit." In his new *tira-han*, the rock musician was still screaming and the electronic guitars were screaming, right into my eardrum. "How many others are there?" I asked, but he would not explain. Instead he snapped at me with another ordinary response, *Don't worry,*

Mom, and when the voices became persistent he closed our conversation and hung up.

"Why is he always so loud?" I said to my friend. "Just because he is far away, does he believe yelling will help?" Francine closed the padded cover of the album and pushed it across the counter, next to my Fry Daddy and a pile of Maribel's overdue bills. "Which do you think is worse," she said, lighting a menthol cigarette. "Boys or girls?" Then she told me about the arguments with her teenage daughters, and we laughed in the quiet afternoon.

"How long's your visit to California?"

Mazi drums his fingers on the steering wheel, waiting for the slow line of automobiles to shrink. The sun has painted the highway in desert colors and I want to escape this boring bus and run between the cars, tapping on windows and waving at the strangers inside.

"I'm not certain. I am surprising my son for his twenty-first birthday." The mid-day heat finds its way through the glass and makes me sweat beneath my arms, this mixture of outside heat and stale air reminding me of the air-conditioned buses I used to ride to Baclaran on Wednesdays, to afternoon Mass, and then to shop for fruit and romance *komiks* in the crowded markets.

"Lucky kid," Mazi says.

"Lucky Mama!"

Above my head in Mazi's wide mirror, only the top half of his face is visible, his dark skin and clear blue eyes, the single dark eyebrow, and I want to reach over his seat and take what is good from his expression and save it for another time.

Mazi grips both hands of the extra-large steering wheel and maneuvers our bus into an outside lane. Is "Lucky Mama" my automatic response? Yes, I want to know if Noel is eating well and studying, if he arrives home safely after his nights out with friends, but unlike my children believe, I do not care about every small detail of their lives. Do I bother to tell them every activity in my day? That I paid two thousand dollars for my new set of dentures? Or that I hate living alone? I fold the peel of my banana and stow it in a plastic baggie inside my bayong. I press my forehead to the cool glass window and notice the boys in the automobile shaking it from side to side. These young men look American. The pale one, the driver, has a red bandanna tied around his scalp and curly locks that poke out from a knot in the back. Their small automobile is like a tarantula, wiggling in the same place with all of the arms and legs dangling outside of the windows. Noel looks American like them, I think; he is taller than his sister Maribel, and he has big bones.

Is this only my perception? To the girls he looks like another Asian boy, I'm sure. I want to say to them, he is *guapo*, my son, can't you see? His nails and his hair grow fast (he always eats rice) and he has dark eyes that do not lie. But this is another of his differences—Noel does not look back at the girls.

When he returned from Stanford after his first semester, a cold December when the snow formed a ramp to the roof of my garage, he did not eat anything at the dinner table, even though I made his favorite—menudo without garbanzo beans. I made a small bowl especially for him; for Maribel and her husband, Thomas, the meat and garbanzos I mixed together.

"Where's your appetite?" I asked him.

"I ate on the plane, Mom."

"*Hay naku,* you eat again." I spooned menudo on his plate of white rice.

Thomas finished his bowl of menudo and gestured (with his mouth full) for Noel's dish. My son-in-law drove thirty-five miles from their horrible house in Lexington to pick Noel up at Logan Airport, so I decided to give him what remained. Both Thomas and Maribel were silent as they ate. Noel drank his water. Were my children extra hungry that night, or, as always, did they have nothing new to say?

I stood and walked to the refrigerator to prepare dessert— vanilla ice cream with coconut shavings, tiny cubes of gelatin, and sweet beans in syrup. From the dining room, I listened as Thomas asked Noel questions about his university. Noel was quiet, answering simply: "Only rain," and "I don't get off campus much."

As I scooped ice cream into individual bowls, I remembered asking Maribel why Noel chose Stanford University over his choices on the East Coast. Maribel said it was because Stanford was Ivy League. But is the Ivy League more important than family? Another evening, when I was babysitting my granddaughter (also named Teresa!), Maribel returned from a date with Thomas and I asked her again. She covered her mouth with her hand and yawned. "Maybe he just wanted to get out, Mom," she said, then carried Teresa to their Jeep, the engine still running, Thomas waiting impatiently in the front seat.

That night I carried the desserts to the table, along with more Pepsi Cola. Noel's plate was no longer steaming. Suddenly he touched my wrist as I poured soda into his glass. He hadn't touched me in this way for years, not since he was a small boy and would swing from my arms with both hands as we waited to see a model of the world at the Christian Science Center. Yes, he hugged me when we said good-bye, or talked to me with his polite tone during our long-distance calls, but not with this true affection.

"Mom, please, sit down."

And after I took my side of our octagonal table and my family was quiet, he told us that he was now a gay. "I've known for a long time," he said. His large hands trembled in his lap.

Did this come from Stanford? I wondered. Would Noel ever get married? I don't know much about being a gay and thought before anything else, *What did I do to make this happen?* I watched as Noel looked to Maribel, who smiled at him across the table. Thomas lowered his head and said nothing. I studied my daughter's expression: in her pressed lips, I saw that she already knew his secret. And so it was my moment, and I took my son's hand and I said, like I think Dr. Phil would say to one of Oprah's weeping guests, "Appearances do not matter," and "I love you no matter who you are."

"Get the hell out of the bus lane!"

Mazi is sweating through the back of his short-sleeved shirt, yelling out his window at the automobile with the rowdy boys. The driver with the pale features puts his arm out his window, gestures at Mazi, and then speeds through the toll booth. Which university do they belong to, Stanford or Berkeley College or the San Francisco School of Art and Design? I learned so many names when Noel was studying the glossy brochures.

I gather my night cream, a disposable camera, and the half-read issues of *Filipinas* magazine on my seat. As I reach to the floor for my runaway ballpoints, I hear Mazi talking with the toll man like they are good friends. The toll man's voice is high-pitched, like a bird, and when I raise myself again, I realize that the toll man is a woman. Our bus continues past many fast-food restaurants and gas stations and I remember my previous journey on this road.

That first trip, we drove from Boston to California in three days, Noel in the driver's seat the entire time. "Every room is wired for the Internet," Noel would say to Maribel in the backseat. Or later, from an expensive guidebook I had given him, "We should visit the Castro—there's lots of good restaurants there." At a Burger King drive-through near Salt Lake City, my baby said: "Did you know Jack Kerouac used to live in San Francisco?" Jack Kerouac was an author who wrote many books, Maribel explained when I asked.

Was Jack Kerouac attracted to other boys like my son? Noel doesn't talk about being a gay. I think he shares these details with Maribel on the telephone, who shares with me only small bits. Once I asked her if there was a chance Noel might marry a nice Filipino girl. "Maybe a boy," she said, making faces at Teresa in her carriage and pretending to pull off her nose.

Another time, when Noel entered junior high school, he came home with his face all red and his fists tightly clenched. *What happened?* I asked, clearing unfinished letters on my bed to make room for him. He sat on the edge of the mattress like a fisherman on a dock. In front of his entire PE class, he explained, the teacher announced he could not play soccer without a jock.

"Marcus Henley told all the girls at school!" Even as a teenager, his hands were always nervous in his lap. I took Maribel aside that evening and gave her twenty dollars and sent them to City Sports. I knew Noel would not go with me. But my Maribel, she was athletic and used to practice her hoop shots long into the night until the shadows from our garage stretched all the way to Francine's back porch. I thought if Maribel offered, Noel would go.

When they returned, Noel stormed by me in the living room without a word. "He was too embarrassed," Maribel said, returning the crumpled bill to my hand. "The saleswoman kept telling him he needed a smaller size."

When we traveled to California that first time, I remembered this story while Noel was unpacking his *damit* in his room. "Did you remember your jockeys?" I asked him, seated on his bare mattress. "You want to fit in with the other boys." And that time we laughed.

Our bus moves along the long boulevard of one-story houses and retail stores, all painted in bright colors. Mazi tells me that we are a few minutes from the San Jose bus terminal. At the station he skillfully steers the bus into a slanted parking space and it bumps to a stop. Through a wall made of windows, many passengers, most of them students, are rushing around, pulling their suitcases behind them on wheels. A woman with a bright scarf tied around her head holds a boy's hand, hurrying him along. She seems to know where she is going.

Before he opens the door, before he allows any of us to step off the bus, Mazi turns in his seat and asks me if I need directions. He is a polite young man with a wife and two girls at home.

"Open the door," I say to him. "Let's be on our way."

Dandy

In the summer of 1972, I beat a man and left him—pinstriped shirt bloodied and eyes swollen to purple slits—on a bank of the Muddy River. He was a man I had met in a bar and he'd given me a blow job. I had never laid hands on anyone before that evening, or since.

Years later, teaching English in the same urban university where I'd completed my graduate and post-graduate degrees, I read the roll call for the first meeting of a composition class. The man I had left for near dead beside the Muddy River sat at the far end of the folding table. He made a striking figure, with his shiny hair pomaded and his crisp pinstriped shirt. He was tall, and though he appeared to be my age—in his late fifties—he had the slouching posture of a young man. I don't know if he recognized me then. When I called his name, Oliver Neal, he raised his hand and dangled a yellow handkerchief at me as if he were waving a tiny dinner bell.

*

I extend the same invitation to my students as I do to my colleagues in Comparative Literature—that is, to call me by my first name, George. Our department chair, Sandra Lockwood, a small unassuming woman with blonde streaks in her hair and raisin-like eyes, asks me for more formality. I disagree. In order to command respect, after all, one must also bestow it.

Now I consider myself neither overly masculine, nor blithe and effeminate. I wear black shoes with black belts and own stylish, unusual ties that I wear to department gatherings or late-summer evenings at the Symphony. I am single. I like a full-bodied Cabernet or Shiraz with my dinner, a vintage port (second-label) following dessert (if given the choice between fruit and pastry, ordinarily fruit), and each January, in the monthlong holiday between terms, I retire to the same vineyard north of San Francisco to escape the brutality of the New England winter. My parents died more than a decade ago, and my nineteen-year-old daughter, Maggie, is my only family besides a few aunts and uncles, second cousins and the like, scattered through the verdant Green Mountains of Vermont.

Oliver Neal, on the other hand, was nothing less than flamboyant. Flamboyant in the manner of Quentin Crisp, complete with witticisms and caustic remarks. One morning I recall that he appeared in class dressed in a tangerine shirt with petal-like frills at the end of the sleeves. It was a "Fight Ugliness" morning, he announced to the class, who, en masse, chuckled. And in a strange way, I found this flamboyance a comfort. Because despite my years of teaching, and Sandra's complaints of my overfamiliarity with students, I retained a certain nervousness when speaking to them. I'd sit in my office before class and jot down notes on lined cards: *Take attendance. Tell joke.* Oliver, in his carefree way, provided a contrast to my nervousness. If I faltered or said things that seemed inane, I would never be as ridiculous as this man.

The first assignment I gave the class was to write two pages about the most frightening event that had occurred to them. It was the same exercise I assigned at the beginning of each term; I found it useful in assessing skills.

As a windy rain clinked the flagpole outside our classroom, the usual parade of eighteen-year-old woes were read aloud: the loss of a sporting event, mutilated romance, the sudden death of a grandparent. Oliver had titled his essay, "The Irreparable Loss of Mr. Cat."

How to be gentle about a dead cat. I placed my bifocals on my forehead and praised the detail of Mr. Cat's sleeping bag, its connotations of warmth and intimacy. It was the easiest part to extrapolate. I talked about the compassion in the essay, how Oliver made the detritus of his tragedy compelling, how he evoked loss without idling in love. Then I commented on the need for organization, several dead metaphors, and a page of descriptions that might be cut.

After I dismissed the class, Oliver remained. He sat with his head erect and hands clasped atop his leather notebook. I was the first to speak: "You're a returning student, Oliver?" This term I'd learned from Sandra. It was a polite way of referring to an older student, the middle-aged housewife or one of a dozen senior citizens in the department's Evergreen program. Oliver smiled. His tanned face seemed to breathe in the sunlight that had displaced the rainstorm and now cast the room in a bland yellow haze.

"I wrote another essay," Oliver said. "The most frightening event that ever happened to me. It was the night I was nearly beaten to death."

He stared at me across the table. I gathered my notes and neatened them like a deck of cards. Was he playing games? Did he recognize me? The morning after I deserted him on the Muddy River, I remember clipping an article from the Globe about the incident and carefully stowing it in a desk drawer. When I discovered it later I stuffed it in my pocket and brought it home, shredding it alongside a leftover cassoulet in the garbage disposal.

Outside my classroom, a young man with a bullhorn blared. The day had brightened considerably. I encouraged Oliver to bring his essay to a future class, speaking with the breezy, non-committal tone of a teacher. (Granted, a part of me was intrigued by his account of that night.) The young man with the bullhorn extolled the virtues of his fraternity to the entire quad.

Oliver stood. His chair scraped the tile floor. With one hand, he carefully smoothed a lock of white hair that had fallen across his cheek. As he closed the door of the classroom, I swore that he winked at me; it seemed as intimate and as flagrant as the handkerchief that he always held in one hand.

*

When I teach, I often assign my students Homer and Dante or the Heaney translation of *Beowulf;* Faulkner or Hemingway if they seem particularly earnest or unread. In the eighth circle of the *Inferno,* for example, Dante is both repelled and fascinated by a pair of disembodied heads, the soul on top making a banquet of the one beneath. It seems an apt metaphor for this life: conquer or be conquered; eat, or be consumed by a voracious beast. Never to this extreme, of course, but I do believe much can be gained from assertiveness.

I follow a Tuesday–Thursday schedule for teaching, and thus slot my office hours to coincide with my days on campus. After our tense conversation, Oliver left a copy of his essay about our Muddy River encounter in my faculty mailbox. A note written on elegant stationary with the initials O. N. embossed on the front accompanied it.

Dear George,

Attached is the story of the most frightening night of my life. I think you will find it revealing. I plan to attend your next office hours and look forward to your reaction.

Respectfully,
Oliver Neal

There was no mention of me in "Under the Bridge," simply the fact that Oliver had never found his assailant. And though the essay's overall tone was one of anger, it was the quietness in his prose that shocked me: the persistent need for closure, the gentle hint of a refrain. There was a natural cadence that seemed to repeat, *Tomorrow, I'll understand,* or the following day, or the next. I was sure he knew my identity and this essay was his method of confrontation. *Come out with it,* I wanted to say, correcting his grammar with a red pen.

On Tuesday morning, Oliver waited in the dim hallway outside my office. He was dressed in a button-down shirt and a gaudy pink tie. I unlocked my door and offered him the chair opposite my own.

"Did you read my essay?" he asked.

I nodded and placed my satchel on the floor.

"It was you. You were the one, George."

I sat quietly and forced myself not to speak.

Oliver leaned forward, elbows on his knees. "That part about leading me out of the reeds? Do you remember that? When we went under the bridge. Me crouching at your waist and undoing your belt—"

"What do you want, Oliver?"

He leaned back, crossing his legs and staring at me. He was pleased with himself, a crooked smile that indicated the distance between student and teacher had been breached. He stared at the floor and I noticed the shiny gloss of scalp beneath his thinning hair. His fingers were pressed together at the tips, resembling an A-frame. Another moment passed and he reached for his brief-case—a rigid brown box—and placed it on his lap. The lid snapped open. Papers, I thought, a lawsuit or some other form of extortion. This, I realized, would please Oliver Neal the most.

He handed me an ordinary file folder with five or six papers inside. I moved my bifocals from my head to my nose and opened the folder. At the top of the first page was the logo and address for Random House Publishers, New York. Below, a letter to Oliver from an acquisitions editor named Marilyn O'Connor.

"I received fifteen thousand dollars up front, because they loved my proposal. The rest of my advance is contingent upon acceptance of the manuscript." Oliver gently closed the lid of his briefcase. "They think it needs structure. Ms. Connor suggested I find an editor, someone with experience. She mentioned a grammar Nazi or some college-type."

He placed his elbows on the armrests of the chair. My chest felt constricted, my teeth unnaturally clenched, but I would not reveal this to Oliver. A part of me began to understand his motivation for enrolling in my composition class.

I leaned back in my desk chair. It creaked loudly: a single, rust-corroded hinge. Oliver was silent, his mouth curved into a thin smile. Much like the old chair, he seemed to squeal with delight.

*

Retribution has always held more interest for me than redemption. Dante? The great poet didn't make lemonade from his lemons. Rather, he squeezed every last drop of acid from the experience and, through his unholy *Inferno,* threw it on the open sores of his persecutors. Twenty-eight years ago, I committed a crime that had yet to be paid for. Now Charon—in the form of a flamboyant middle-aged dandy—had arrived to ferry me across the river.

Several days later, I sat in my office and reread Oliver's manuscript. He had written approximately eighty pages of his life story, a description of his childhood in a wealthy Boston suburb to his melodramatic sixteenth birthday, when he entered his family's parlor in white bloomers and one of his mother's strapless sundresses. His father, a staunch New England Brahmin, smacked him, and his mother locked herself in their solarium and wept.

"How could you do this to us?" Father fumed. He yanked Mother's beautiful sundress off me and I stood before him in the parlor, naked as the wind.

"You don't understand," I yelled back, piercing him like a razor-sharp blade. "And you never will. I'm not like you. I will never be so old." (Did Oliver mean "bold"? or "cold"?)

That was the last time I spoke with Father. Like a fragile bouquet that has bloomed and lost its fragrant scent, my dear Father died later that same day.

Oliver's manuscript was riddled with this florid prose. I'd read better descriptions of bat mitzvahs and seventh grade dances.

We discussed revision strategies and new ideas for the manuscript on a weekly basis. In the beginning I wrote minimal comments on the manuscript and dreaded the endless recall of that evening. I wanted to refuse him altogether, but Oliver had intoned, however subtly, that he had no qualms about contacting the police. One cold October morning, we talked quietly in my office, the high-pitched clanking of the radiator a counterpoint to our quiet conversation. Oliver had written a description of our fateful encounter that paralleled the tale of David and Goliath.

And there went out a Goliath that lured me carefully into the reeds. I was enthralled by this monster, being but a young and defenseless David, and I would have followed him anywhere. I was portrayed as a vicious, one-dimensional beast and Oliver the noble though disadvantaged David.

I handed him a sheet with my comments organized in a bulleted list. "Can't we tone down the aggression a bit?" I asked. "Make the monster more human?"

Oliver snorted. "The entire story hinges on your aggression, George."

"But you *asked* me to hit you." There was a surreal quality to our conversation, as if we were discussing gardening rather than a violent encounter. I tapped my shoe restlessly on the floor beneath my desk.

"That's irrelevant, isn't it? I want this to be fierce, to embody the wild terror I felt that night. It must be epic, George! 'He who desires, but acts not, breeds pestilence.' Oscar Wilde said that."

Of course Oliver chose to identify with Wilde. I didn't tell him the quotation sounded more like William Blake.

I swallowed and straightened my dark tie. "The reader has to feel sympathy for *both* characters, Oliver. You need to prepare us for the confrontation. It will only make the story more resonant." I looked at him directly in the face.

Oliver made a constipated expression, his upper lip touching the end of his nose. For a moment I considered suggesting a composition handbook I preferred that emphasized the audience as a focusing force.

"I know what you want me to say, George. But this is my story." He grabbed his manuscript from my desk. "I'm going to tell it the way it happened."

*

The second week in October, my daughter, Maggie, phoned. She was in the process of selecting spring classes and had to declare a major. I asked which of her courses interested her.

"I really like Cultural Studies. Don't smirk, George. Somebody needs to deconstruct hip-hop lyrics for old white guys like you." I laughed. In the background, I heard the sizzle of a lighter and I imagined Maggie in her dorm room smoking a cigarette. It pleased me that I was privy to a few secrets that her mother did not know.

"Have you considered a career as an educator?"

"I don't want to be in school forever."

"But you've only been at Princeton a few months! Teaching is more than a few late-night conversations in the dorm. Why don't you observe me while I teach?"

Her birthday was forthcoming, I reminded her, and I hoped that the incentive of a fancy meal would also entice her. I wanted Maggie to accept. My daughter is bright and genial, "not gay, but gay-friendly" I heard her remark once, the kind of young woman who prefers listening to all sides of an argument before making a decision.

"Let me think about it, and I'll let you know. Goodnight, George." I heard the click of her telephone before hanging up the phone. I returned to the dozen or so essays I had yet to grade.

*

Maggie loves literature as much as I do. She has always been a reader—solely my influence, I'd like to believe, but her mother, my friend Pamela (to whom I donated my sperm but with whom have never been romantically involved) was an advocate of Shakespeare and Yeats, Trollope (to my chagrin), as well as the Romantics and even the Beats. Pamela has been a devoted friend since our undergraduate days, when she and I worked for a research lab that studied attention deficit disorders in children; now she is "Dr. Pam" to our friends and practices internal medicine at Brigham and Women's. She has always supported a close relationship between Maggie and myself, explaining to

Maggie when she entered junior high school that I was her birth father. The timing couldn't have been better: Maggie asked me to Sadie Hawkins dances and to offer an impartial ear when her mother would not. But our time together had become increasingly limited during this time, her difficult freshman year. A few days after our phone call, Maggie told me she had purchased a plane ticket to Boston. I immediately began to buy her favorite junk foods—yogurt pretzels and caramel rice cakes—as well as her thick fashion magazines.

Our lesson the Thursday of Maggie's visit was on the persuasive essay. Oliver's manuscript, of course, had usurped much of my time, so I offered up the usual suspects: King's "I Have a Dream" speech, a thoughtful essay on migraines, a brief excerpt from *Notes of a Native Son*. Only two-thirds of my class were in their seats when we arrived.

I introduced Maggie and she sat in a desk chair apart from our table near the window. She produced a reporter's notepad and a pen, and sat poised in her deliberate way. Did we both sense that she wasn't going to learn anything from my class? Her attentiveness—the very effort of it—emboldened me and reminded me of a child seeking approval. Earlier, over breakfast, we had argued about her education and her staunch refusal to accept my financial support. In her gravelly voice she repeated, *I'll pay for it myself, George, or I just won't go.* Last spring she had entertained the idea of working on a fishing boat in Alaska with her deadbeat boyfriend rather than enter Princeton. Pamela and I tried to be gentle in our disapproval, but it was her boyfriend's dull lack of adventure that ultimately changed her mind.

Oliver, of course, volunteered to read his essay aloud; it was an excerpt from a chapter we'd just revised in conference.

Ostensibly, the topic was the formative years of the homosexual. "Nature or nurture?" he began, and I felt the physical attentiveness of my students like a musician who intuits his audience from the stage. Maggie, too, leaned forward in her rickety chair.

"The homosexual has always been oppressed in society. This essay seeks to understand why this oppression occurs—but more importantly, the roots of homosexual desire." I recognized the passage from the end of chapter eight.

Oliver gestured theatrically. I caught Maggie's eye and she shrugged. It seemed more an acknowledgment of Oliver's essay topic than a truce to our morning argument. How could I make her understand? Her education was something I valued; it was something I was passionate about and could easily bestow upon her.

"In reality, homosexuals aren't the oppressed," Oliver concluded, "but the oppressors. Until we learn to voice our opinions, to love ourselves, how can we expect others to love us?"

I thought Oliver's argument lacked teeth, and had told him so, but my students applauded, a horde of impressionable freshmen. Oliver had ignored my wishes for more dialogue and scene rather than his long-winded proselytizing. He was a stubborn man. I looked at Maggie in the back of the room, hunched over her reporter's notebook, nodding to no one. What was she puzzling over? Could she still be angry about our morning argument?

I dismissed the class and the usual zippering of bookbags ensued. Maggie approached me and I hugged her around the shoulders, suggesting a restaurant for lunch, but she remained rigid. When Oliver passed us, Maggie tapped him on the shoulder.

"I loved your essay," she said. "Could I read a copy of it?"

Oliver clapped his hands at chest level. "I would be honored, Maggie!" He introduced himself, holding out his left hand, hinged at the wrist, as if he were royalty. Maggie clasped it warmly.

"You must be proud of your father," Oliver said. "He's a *fabulous* tutor."

They turned and looked at me. Maggie's eyes narrowed.

I fastened the brass buckle of my satchel, staring at my daughter. She was still angry with me. Oliver continued to rant about our special relationship, then asked Maggie how long she was visiting me. Their banter—the easy familiarity—frustrated me but I tried to play along. After a few minutes I held Maggie's elbow and whispered, "Let's hurry, honey. I want to beat the lunch crowd on Newbury Street."

Maggie looked at Oliver. She seemed to sense my impatience and shook me off, linking arms with Oliver. "Why don't you join us? We're celebrating my birthday today. George shouldn't be my only guest."

*

The crowded restaurant Maggie had chosen was not on Newbury Street as I had hoped but rather in Kenmore Square, and was decorated with a car wash–style banner, a depressing mural of a fiesta, and a fireplace containing a television monitor—which in turn played a videotape of a crackling fire. The specialties were slow-cooked barbecue brisket and lime-green margaritas. Our waiter, a laconic young man in no particular hurry, approached our table and stared at me in a direct manner for several seconds.

"Remember me, George? I wrote the essay about the karaoke tournament I won in junior high?"

"Of course," I lied. He stretched his arm in the air like a basketball player, awaiting my slap. I lowered it and shook his hand.

The waiter, Rudy, sat unexpectedly in my booth and wrote down our drink order: a vodka martini for me, a Diet Coke for Maggie, and, for Oliver, the house margarita. As he walked away, I told Maggie and Oliver that his writing was remarkable only for his overuse of semicolons.

Maggie unrolled her napkin, chiding me. She leaned into Oliver. "Do you really think my father's a good teacher?"

"I'm being humble when I say that George is quite remarkable. He has always encouraged me to write the truth." With his yellow handkerchief in the air, he winked at me.

I returned his confidence with a frown, smoothing my napkin in my lap.

"Good," Maggie said. "Because he's trying to convince me to follow in his footsteps."

There was an awkward silence. Oliver dipped a tortilla chip in salsa. I wondered if he had the gall to reveal our relationship to her.

Maggie said, "Your essay made a good argument for nature, Oliver, but I'm not sure it's necessarily true."

"Let's not discuss this right now," I said.

She fastened her eyes on me.

"It's *my* party, isn't it?" She turned to Oliver. "Did you ever lie to anybody about yourself?"

I tapped Oliver's boot beneath the table, trying to silence him with a glance. "My dear," he said, "I told my parents the terrible truth about their son when I turned sixteen."

"Really? How did they take it?"

"My mother threw a tantrum. And then my father had a heart attack."

Maggie's mouth dropped and she expressed her sympathies. Again she turned to me and asked the same question. I ignored her, staring at the electronic flame across the room. Oliver sipped his lime-green margarita. I was willing to wait out the silence, but Oliver could not. He politely excused himself to the bathroom.

"You don't have to be so uptight," Maggie said.

"How could you invite him? This was supposed to be our celebration."

"I'm sick of arguing with you all the time."

I reached out and held her soft fingers atop the table. Her nails were painted a glossy white. "What can I do to please you, Maggie?"

"Just lighten up." She pulled her hand away. "Why can't you be more like Oliver?"

I crumpled my napkin beneath the table. "Oliver Neal is not a role model."

"I like him. He's got a good sense of humor."

He's a dandy, I wanted to yell, but held my tongue. What kind of man would I be if I carried myself like him? Maggie craned her neck to where Oliver had disappeared behind an old pair of saloon doors.

She turned to me, her mouth pulled back at the corners. "It's obvious you hate him."

For a brief instant I wanted to tell her the truth. I wanted
her to know about Oliver's cunning, his manipulation of me and
his book deal. I wanted her to know that Oliver consented to
everything that night beside the Muddy River. Over her shoulder, I saw Oliver talking near the restroom with Rudy. He had
twisted his arm to show Oliver an intricate tattoo that circled its
upper half. Oliver squeezed his bicep and cooed.

Maggie stared out the large plate-glass window.

"If you're ever to be an educator, a truly exceptional one,"
I said, "you must understand that teachers and students don't
mix. It's asking for trouble. I hope you can understand."

She gave a weary sigh. When Oliver slid back into the padded booth, he unfolded a receipt and showed it to her. It was not
until a few days later, when I dropped my daughter at Logan
Airport, that she shared the contents. Rudy had given Oliver his
phone number and, below it, reduced the bill for Maggie's birthday dinner by thirty percent.

*

Later that autumn, Pamela made plans for a cruise to the
Bahamas with her partner. Maggie and I decided to celebrate
the Thanksgiving holiday in my home. Oliver had quickly put
together a passable first draft, two-hundred-odd pages, and left
it for me in my faculty mailbox before the holiday break began.
It had finally become exciting, working on our book, and I had
convinced myself that the story was not the actual event, but
a dramatization. Years of deconstructing Eliot and Pound had
taught me to separate the writer from the text. Our meetings
centered on Oliver's voice, the diction, his occasional lapses of

tone. He had surprised me with his professionalism and determined approach.

Maggie sat in my kitchen on Thanksgiving morning and read a tattered copy of *Vogue*. I cracked three eggs on the rim of a stainless steel bowl.

"There's an article here by a gay kid—I mean, the child of a gay couple. The interviewer asked him if he had a choice, who would he pick? Straight or gay parents? Guess how he answered."

"God forbid." I placed her toast on a porcelain plate and slid it along with a small jar of marmalade across the counter.

"Gay, of course. Isn't that awesome?"

"A feel-good article. No one, of course, would *choose* gay parents."

Maggie frowned, buttering her toast. The eggs congealed in an old frying pan on the stove. Maybe her mother never should have told Maggie my identity. I think it may have been too much for any young girl.

"You're just so cynical, George. My roommate says pessimism is bad for your skin." She took her toast and her magazine and sprawled on my Turkish carpet. I sighed. Maggie's new bravado: she reminded me of one of my students.

The telephone rang and Maggie looked at me. I ignored both, breaking the egg yolk in the pan. When the answering machine picked up, Oliver spoke. "I was thinking we should work on the sex scene, George. Do you think it's too graphic? Maybe we should make my attacker immediately regret hitting me. Just a thought. Ciao."

I slid the fried eggs to another plate. Maggie raised her dark eyebrows at me. I feigned interest in the sports section of the

Globe, and when I failed to acknowledge her, she rose, touching my forearm, giving up on a response.

"Did you know Mom wanted me to go to Grandma's house for Thanksgiving?" She sat on a high stool across from me at the counter. "She thinks your issues will rub off on me. I said, 'What issues?' but she wouldn't say."

Maggie laid her hand flat on the newspaper headline that I was reading. "Why can't we just talk like regular people, George?"

I stared at her delicate fingers. Though I loved Maggie and would support her unconditionally, I was unwilling to share this part of my life. How could I possibly broach it? How could I explain to her that Oliver Neal had once engaged me in anonymous sex and then asked me to strike him under the Boylston Street bridge?

I was her father. Yet I didn't want to invoke this cliché.

"Maggie, please," I said, placing my hand on top of hers. "Allow me to keep parts of my life private." What I did with other men, whom I chose to be physically intimate with, was of no concern to her.

She slinked to the bathroom as if she'd been reprimanded (or, upon reflection, hurt). I didn't know how to comfort her. She would spend the rest of that weekend talking to her mother long-distance, prodding me with existential questions, drinking coffee. Always, *always,* trying to steer the conversation to the topic of sexuality. *My* sexuality, *my* unwillingness to talk about it. She was infuriating. Watching her now, sulking from my living room to the bathroom, she was simply my nineteen-year-old daughter, impressionable and idealistic in her white polished nails, still hopeful of change in this world.

I heard the click of the bathroom door. I gathered her dirty plate and rinsed the remains of her toast in the sink.

*

Arnold, the manager at Devon's, filled a highball glass with plain-label gin and tonic water, then ran a thin lime wedge along the rim. I had dropped Maggie at Logan Airport with a small crate of tangerines and twenty minutes to spare before her flight back to New Jersey.

"My bartender called in sick for the third time this week. Can you believe it, George?" He set the drink before me. Despite his complaint, Arnold was smiling. I imagined that pouring cocktails in the crowded bar was better than paying invoices in his dingy office, surrounded by cases of beer and a metal desk where late one drunken night he had lowered my trousers and I had allowed him to pleasure me.

Arnold lifted my gin and tonic from the bar and set a small napkin below it. I stirred the petite red straw and then sucked the gin from the end. Devon's was crowded with bare-chested men in leather pants and matching leather caps. There were a few put-together college students who talked in small tribes at high tables.

"Why so glum?"

"Oh, Arnold," I said, "my daughter loathes me."

He leaned on his chin and poured himself a Coke from the soda nozzle.

"Things can only get better."

Arnold struck me as a "good old" type—welcoming to everyone, discriminating against no one. I'd always found it surprising, the fraternity of a gay establishment. Community newspapers and support group flyers near the door, disco music blaring from mounted speakers, men cruising other men but also laughing with one another and greeting each other with kisses on the mouth.

Arnold nodded in the direction of the jukebox. "That boy in the corner? He's got a sweet smile for you."

I turned. The stocky red-haired boy looked barely out of high school. A Red Sox cap was level with his eyebrows and he possessed a shy, unassuming smile. Dimples fast at work. He was seated at a table with two equally youthful friends.

"Thank you, Arnold, but he looks like one of my students." I finished my drink and then walked away from the bar to the billiards table. The red-haired boy's gaze followed me. Soon he stood and went to the bathroom. I followed him, standing at the stall to his right. "What's your name?" I asked.

He smiled. "Chad."

We moved to the porcelain sinks and I introduced myself. Chad rubbed his hands beneath the faucet and then combed his wet fingers through his short hair.

"You don't look of age, Chad."

"How old do you think I am?"

"About sixteen."

"It's the zits. I just moved back from California. Do you know how much LA revolves around sex?"

I laughed, asking him if he'd like to have a nightcap. On the short walk to my apartment he told me his life story: he had attended a private school in Cambridge, then, upon graduation, moved to Los Angeles to pursue acting. His accomplishments over the past three years, however, consisted of a diet soda commercial and a management position at a pornography shop in West Hollywood. I encouraged him to keep at it, as I would with any of my students. "It's difficult to wend one's way through the Inferno," I added.

Half an hour later, inside my disorderly living room, I handed him a bottle of beer and told him to remove his baseball cap, make himself at home. He flashed that quick smile I noticed at Devon's, and said he'd remove whatever I wanted.

Truthfully, boys did nothing for me. It was body hair I loved, the goatee circling a man's lips, the muscular thighs, the soft scratch of hair beneath the arms. These things aroused me and reminded me I was with another man. If I wanted smooth skin, I would have made love to women. When I removed Chad's shirt, the zits he'd mentioned in the bar covered his shoulders and back like small red ants.

When he was unclothed, he crouched in front of me at my piano bench and removed my loafers. He reached for my waist and I helped him to remove my black belt, my dark linen trousers, my boxers. He threw my trousers on top of the piano. I wanted to fold them neatly. Instead I ran my hand through his short red hair, and he looked up, asked what I wanted to do.

"Hit me," I said, somewhat uncertainly.

"I'm sorry?"

I kissed him and then handed him my belt. "With this." His red lips were parted, not sure how to proceed; I grinned, noting that he was aroused.

Except for laying hands on Oliver Neal nearly three decades earlier, I can say that I have never struck, or been struck, by another man. Chad rose to his feet and gathered his clothes from the patterned settee where they lay. I remained seated on the piano bench.

As he dressed, I repeated my request.

Chad shook his head, incredulous. He began to button his pants. "You're fucked up," he said, lifting my trousers off the piano and hurling them at me. He squared his Red Sox cap on his head. "What's that word for a crazy old queen?"

Before I could reply he had unlocked the dead bolt. He let himself out the door.

Good Men

The bar had been packed away. Outside, behind the huge reception tent, the waitstaff sat on plastic coolers and smoked Marlboro Lights. They laughed and gestured, the lit ends of their cigarettes glowing in the darkness like fireflies. Bottles clinked to her right, and Clea spied Walt near an old pickup truck sorting empties.

She approached him, smiling. "You're not leaving, are you?"

"When the alcohol's gone, I am, too."

She hadn't realized it was so late. The heft of evening had been shut out of the loud tent. In the cool Atlantic air she sobered quickly, as if she'd walked into a bright hospital waiting room. Her shock was mild in comparison to the day's events: nothing could top the low-pitched voice of her ex-boyfriend, Noel, reciting his wedding vows to another man.

Walt poured leftover beer from a bottle to the ground. Relieved of his bartending duties, he'd covered his bald head with a fisherman's hat.

"So, what now?" she asked, hands on her hips.

He smiled, shaking his head. "You city people. Always moving so fast."

She wasn't sure if he was talking about her forwardness or some physical trait, maybe the way she was rolling from heels to toes, backward and forward, hands clasped behind her back.

"Take me for a ride."

"What about your friend?"

"Hugo's a big boy. Anyway, he's going back to the B&B to nurse a headache."

Walt lifted the last case of bottles into the back of his truck. "I've gotta get rid of these; that's the extent of my evening." He closed the gate with an upward shove then climbed into the cab. Clea waited. A tiny safety pin at the hem of her dress scratched at her thigh. The pickup's engine turned three times before it started and Walt opened the passenger door, leaning out.

"Well," he asked, "you coming or not?"

*

The winding rural roads leading from the coast of Maine to the inland towns were even darker than the leafy grounds of the reception. Clea watched the spruce trees blur and bend toward Walt's pickup, the bright moon to the west leaning its chin on the horizon. The smell of fresh-cut grass, carried on the night breeze, felt like someone blowing on her face. The evening felt like a secret. Walt seemed to be driving to the furthest point from the lobster pounds and mini-golf courses she'd seen lining the coastal road from Kittery to Kennebunkport on the drive up from Boston. She'd flirted with him behind the bar for most of the evening because the wedding of Noel had become too sober-ing, the grin she'd adopted too constricting—like too much time in a tightly fitted bra. She and Noel were still friends, but no matter how mature she wanted to be, she felt ridiculous attend-ing his gay wedding. Hugo had corrected her on the drive up: Noel's *commitment ceremony*. She wished he hadn't encouraged her to be his date.

Walt seemed intelligent, and he had handsome blue eyes. With every gin and tonic she ordered at the reception, she'd learned more about him: that he was thirty-four years old (six years older than her), and at an early age was naturally bald—*in a becoming way,* she had teased him. He wore a thin, waxed mustache that curled up at the ends like two miniature arms flexing their biceps. It was her first trip to Maine, and she was happy to discover it wasn't overrun by the rednecks and wealthy New Englanders she'd imagined. Clea had grown up on Maui and moved to the mainland ten years earlier to attend Stanford. Her friends, most of whom had migrated to Boston after college, still teased her with the nickname *Hula Girl* and liked to shout, "Aloha, Clea!" when they met at the same smoky bar on Friday nights. Maine had a deep, sultry feel that reminded her of home—cooler, of course, and earthier.

"You must hate tourists."

"They're good for the economy. People like it here, rent houses for the summer and then stay, buy places along the shore." He propped his arm in the open window and cupped the breeze. "Means more business for me, I guess, all those sun-porches and extra rooms." Walt earned his living as a contractor, sometimes moonlighting as a bartender for extra cash.

He pushed in the black knob of the truck's lighter and fished in his shirt pocket for cigarettes. Clea watched, noticing his callused fingers and short bitten nails. No rings. An ex-wife, she imagined, but probably no girlfriend.

The treaded tires vibrated over the grate of a long bridge. Walt lit a cigarette without offering one to Clea. How did he know she didn't smoke? Below them, she caught the beam of a flashlight roving the riverbank and then skimming the calm surface of the water. Walt turned the radio on, probably for her benefit, tuning it to various rock stations before switching it off.

Clea leaned against her door. "Doesn't all this quiet drive you nuts?"

He didn't answer, blowing a thin stream of smoke out the window. Clea was annoyed but checked herself, trying to match his composure. What was it that allowed men to tune out, like an infant asleep in a crowded restaurant? She stared at the tall trees, the cloudy, moonlit sky. For several miles she watched the dotted white line of the road, eventually forgetting his silent affront. Her thoughts drifted to Noel, the disappointment she'd felt as she watched his face light up at the reception while he talked to Chad (was he now called Noel's *husband?*) and his sister, Maribel. Walt turned off the road into a hidden driveway, the tires crunching loudly on gravel. His cabin was set back about a mile from the road in a large clearing ringed by fir trees. For a moment she worried about her absence from the afterparty, but then decided she would make up an excuse.

Walt parked his truck on a patch of dry grass. "Come on, I'll make us something to eat."

The inside of his cabin was sparsely furnished, a ratty carpet, a couch, a large-screen television to the left of a large picture window. She felt confident no woman had ever shared this house. He opened the refrigerator and removed a carton of eggs and two cans of Budweiser, handing one to Clea. She leaned on the counter in front of the sink. "So, which of those guys get-ting married was your friend?" he asked.

"Both of them. But the Filipino one used to be my boyfriend."

Walt nodded, making a sound like *hmmm*. He removed his fisherman's hat and placed it on the counter. His head shone in the moonlight that slanted through one of the skylights. Walt moved up to her and Clea thought he was going to kiss her, but he reached for a frying pan on the shelf above her head. She liked the smell of alcohol and starch on his tuxedo shirt as he stretched against her, and she wanted to put her hands around his waist, remove his clothes and her dress right there in the middle of the kitchen. It had been more than a year since she'd been with Noel or anyone else—twelve-plus months, and her ex-boyfriend had not only come out of the closet, but also married the man of his dreams. Why hadn't she? Hugo had dutifully tried to console her, telling her it was all material for her book; now, he had said, grinning, she could write a trashy memoir about how she had managed to turn her boyfriend gay.

Walt set the frying pan on the stove. She glanced at a wire sculpture on the window ledge above the sink. Two figures were balanced on a teeter-totter. She reached out and set it in motion.

"That must have been hard for you," Walt said. He turned on the gas stove and the petal-like flames formed a blue flower.

"My friend Hugo says all the good men are gay." She rubbed the upper half of her arms though she wasn't cold. She felt a second wind, in fact, alert and somewhat playful. "Maybe we could save some time. You're not a closet case, are you?"

Walt laughed. He cracked four eggs and let them fry in the pan. Clea wondered if breakfast before sex meant he wasn't interested in her, or if he was just hungry. She wanted him to cook again in the morning.

"I've never tried it, but I'm pretty sure I prefer women. You?"

"My mother leaves these messages on my machine. 'Clea, this is Mommy. Are you a gay?' I play them for Hugo and we crack up." She twisted the tab off her Budweiser can. "I think Noel and I met before he had a chance to figure things out."

Walt finished cooking and handed her the eggs on a cracked plate. He gently pushed the screen door open with one heel. Clea followed. They sat on a picnic table facing the woods and a wide path that had been trampled to the lake. The breeze carried the clean smell of the forest, and Clea listened to the croaking of frogs, which sounded as if they were being broadcast over loudspeakers somewhere in the bushes. The summer leaves rustled, and she pictured herself lying in Walt's bedroom, listening to these sounds instead of the drunk students who screamed obscenities outside her ground-floor apartment in Allston at night.

Walt tapped her knee and pointed to the right.

Thirty feet away, a rusty oil barrel had been cut in half and set above the ground on two sawhorses. Grazing from the makeshift trough was a small moose. Its intricate antlers looked fake, like a coatrack at the restaurant where Clea worked. She moved closer to him on the table, her shoulder pressing into his side, and he wrapped his arm around her. The animal lifted its head at the sound of the table's creaking, then, unmoved, returned to its feeding. She whispered in his ear, asking if the moose would attack them.

Walt laughed. "It's a white-tailed deer." He explained that a family of them lived in the woods surrounding his cabin. One day on a whim he'd built the trough, wondering if they'd come near it.

Above them the fiberglass clouds thinned and a sickle of moon hung in the sky. The deer finished its meal and bounded in the opposite direction.

"I should get back," Clea said, stretching her arms.

Walt sucked in his lips, as if he'd removed a pair of dentures. He looked at her, then down at his boots. "You could stay." His thin moustache crooked at a comic angle.

She leaned into him again and pulled his arm around her. After a while they stood. He held out a callused hand and led her inside.

*

Clea wiggled out of her crushed velvet dress. She sat on the quilt strewn across his bed in her panties while Walt removed his tuxedo shirt. She reached up to his neck and then his broad shoulders, running her nails through the curly hair covering his chest. His body was taut and muscled. Soon she was holding the waist of his trousers while he stepped out of them, discovering that he wasn't aroused.

Walt stood before her in his white briefs. "I want you," he said, explaining. "It's just been a long day."

Clea huddled beneath the quilt and pulled it up to her chin. He lay down gently beside her. Here is another man, she thought, not attracted to me. She wanted to tell him that it was okay, that they would just sleep, and in her mind he agreed. But didn't that defeat the notion of a one-night stand? Spooning would be a disappointment.

She turned away from him and faced the bare window. He moved closer to her, barely touching, and then lifted her long hair, draping it above her head on the pillow. He kissed her shoulders, *One for each freckle,* he whispered, and his moustache felt like an eyeliner brush raking her skin. He pressed against her back, and she knew that he was hard.

She turned to him and ran her knuckles lightly over his stubbled cheek.

"Momentary setback," he said, covering her hand with his. Clea kissed him and they made love.

*

The following morning, Clea and Hugo sped down Route 1. Hugo drove the rental car twenty miles over the speed limit, past Ogunquit and Kittery into New Hampshire. Boston was less than an hour away. She had just recounted her evening to him, and Hugo asked if she planned to see the bartender again.

"I don't think so," Clea said. "We didn't say."

Walt had written his home number on the back of his business card and handed it to her that morning, but Clea hadn't exchanged hers. Now she regretted the decision. If Walt had been offended, he didn't show it. He waved to her as he backed his old pickup down the B&B's driveway, and she turned and climbed the front steps. Inside, beneath the living room arch, she thought she had forgotten something at his cabin in the woods. But she was wrong; she hadn't taken anything to the wedding except a few bills pinned to the inseam of her black dress. She felt along her thick hem and found the safety pins and the money in the same place. She laughed to herself. In the rush of last night's events, she'd forgotten her usual concerns.

Now she unrolled the window of the rental car. Hot July air rushed in from the highway while Hugo babbled about the simplicity of Noel's commitment ceremony, how happy he looked. Clea nodded, closing her eyes. She wanted Hugo to stop talking. She wanted to remember the clink of bottles outside the reception, the smell of grass along the rural roads, the way Walt's kisses felt on her bare shoulders. She wanted to remember the expression of her white-tailed deer.

Babies

More incredible things had happened, Hugo thought, than a man giving birth. Frogs were born with six limbs; praying mantises laid eggs in gummy lines, backtracked, and then ate them like licorice. It was the last late evening of summer and Hugo propped his pillow up in bed, copyediting a piece about the equinox.

"I want to get pregnant," Hugo said, placing his hand idly on Mitchell's head. Earlier that day, in the crowded newsroom, a freckled intern had seen a push-pinned photo of him and Mitchell and remarked that they would have the most beautiful children.

Mitch pushed Hugo's hand away. "You're kidding, right?" He placed his thin spectacles on a stack of milk crates—Hugo's idea of a night table. "Reality to Planet Hugo? We can barely pay our mortgage and now you want a child?"

Did the serious ever laugh? Mitch slid off the bed and removed his sweatpants. His boyfriend liked to worry about the quotidian things in life, repointing the bricks of their crumbling brownstone or toning his svelte, thirty-four-year-old body. In the world of respectable people, Mitch was a freelance nutritionist. *Health,* he liked to repeat to Hugo, *is more noble than science. Your body is a temple.* Hugo outwardly agreed, keeping to himself the knowledge that biology was fundamental to Mitch's vain world of nutrition.

Science, on the other hand, was Hugo's hummus and pita bread. He lay against their headboard and smoothed the velvety nap of the blanket. It wasn't child-rearing or adoption Hugo craved (he hadn't thought that far ahead), but the actual creation of human life. His and Mitch's baby! He laughed, lifting his papers and imagining a baby with Mitch's pepper-gray hair and his own straw-colored skin.

Mitch locked in his plastic mouthguard and closed his eyes. In a minute he was snoring. Hugo set his papers aside and watched his boyfriend sleep, and then turned off his lamp. He lay motionless on his back, feeling the leafy shadows from outside shimmer on the painted walls. The room was like a giant aquarium.

Slowly the blanket floated off him, billowing in the room of blue-black water. He, too, floated up from the bed, reaching his hands to his neck and touching the flaky gills beneath his chin. Light waves splashed the stucco ceiling, and a few fathoms below, Hugo could see the black silt collecting on his computer monitor and along the crevices of the wide hardwood planks.

Hugo spread out his arms and kicked lightly, looking down at Mitchell in their neat bed. He exhaled an upward-arching stream of bubbles. If male insects could make babies, he wondered, why couldn't he?

*

He'd met Mitchell on a panel titled, "Nuts for Nutrition: Why Saturated Fat is Good for You." Mitchell was the moderator, then a graduate student from Georgetown who asked easy questions of the well-known scientists and funneled the unanswerable ones to Hugo, an editor for a basement-operation journal. Mitchell approached him later over a tray of rolled deli meat and pickle spears. "You throw me curveballs in front of the audience," Hugo said, "and then flirt with me during the reception."

Mitchell fumbled with his paper plate, a black olive rolling off the edge. "I hope you don't think I was sabotaging you," he stammered. "I mean, it doesn't matter who you are. It's what you bring to the table."

Hugo listened patiently, watching Mitch's biceps tighten in his short-sleeved dress shirt. Mitchell lived in DC and was in town to volunteer for the conference. When the reception dwindled he invited Hugo for a drink at the hotel bar. Three vodka martinis led to a nightcap in Mitchell's hotel room, sloppy kisses on the cold balcony overlooking Boston Harbor, and sex with the television tuned to scrolling hotel announcements. For half a year he and Mitchell emailed every day, and once a month one picked the other up at the Delta Shuttle gate. On a whim Hugo sent Mitchell a script he'd written for phone sex.

They gave up after the first ridiculous attempt, Hugo losing it at Mitchell's dry intonation of the words "love meat."

Hugo's nine-year-old niece, Evelina, had visited for Christmas, coinciding with one of Mitchell's stays. When Mitch suggested they bring her to the Museum of Science, Hugo said, "Why not the orthodontist? She could drop in for a quick root canal."

They brought her instead to a touring production of *Hairspray,* explaining as they waited in line before the performance that it—the show—was their Christmas gift to her. "You're kidding, right?" she replied gravely. It had been a running joke ever since.

During the first year Mitchell moved into Hugo's floor-through apartment, their domestic life was like a Van Gogh painting, the madness barely hidden beneath the bright, slathered-on colors. The intensity of their relationship was apparent not only in Mitchell's omelet dinners or their Sunday afternoons at the Museum of Fine Arts, but in their arguments—in the beginning, over small things: unpaid bills, messy closets, sleeping routines. Before long their fights crept into the tenuous territory where insecurity and other men waited.

At work, Hugo began tracking the project of a famous archaeologist in Cairo who was studying the movements of the sun. Each day he measured the length of a ray as it crept across a long cathedral floor, posting his observations on the Web. Hugo bookmarked the site, checking its daily progress. It was just like love: some days the sun blazed with an uncategorical brightness, and other times it crept predictably along its parallax on the marble floor.

When Mitchell began an affair with one of his clients— an Indian architect who ate too much carbs and not enough protein—Hugo felt his anger was half-assed, as if he were upset only because that was how a wronged spouse was supposed to act.

But he wasn't a spouse, was he? Mitchell had argued. *More like a spousal equivalent.* Though they had been dating then for more than three years, Hugo was neither his husband nor his wife. He was, for lack of a better word, his lover. Hugo didn't want to listen to logic. He wanted Mitchell to either end the affair or move out.

Aryana, Hugo's twice-divorced sister, shared her advice for reining in a husband: babies. "It's all about guilt. There's nothing like a kid to keep them at home." He and Mitchell decided to buy a condo instead.

They moved into an eight-unit brownstone with steep front steps that led to the second floor. The matter of Mitch's affair they packed into their cardboard boxes and moved with them. Hugo agreed to an open relationship. *Gay men could do that,* Aryana said, avoiding her brother's gaze, *just sleep around.* And as far as Hugo knew, Mitch was sleeping with half of his clients while he tried to lure Joe the Intern out for a beer. This was the same freckled intern who'd said about him and Mitchell, "You two would have the most beautiful children." He had no idea how prescient he really was.

*

Hugo woke from his aquatic dream feeling nauseated. He rushed to the bathroom, crouched in front of the toilet, and vomited with his eyes shut. Holding the cold wreath of the seat, he remembered the vinegar-tasting salsa Mitch had used to make omelets the previous evening.

He leaned against the porcelain tub and severed the string of saliva from his mouth. Maybe it wasn't the salsa; maybe it was a fever.

"You all right?" Mitch said, staring down at him from the doorway. His gray hair was wild with unintentional bedhead. He wore bikini briefs and a black T-shirt.

"Fine. Those eggs," Hugo said.

"Want some water?"

Hugo leaned forward, crossing his arms on his knees. He wanted to be alone.

"I'm fine, Mitch. Go back to bed." Hugo held the edge of the tub and stood.

Mitch scuffed down the hall to their bedroom. Hugo flushed the toilet. He leaned over their wide scallop of a sink, staring at his complexion in the mirror. His skin was ashy, his eyes gaunt. Was it flu season? The term was ridiculous, like all the metaphorical seasons: allergy season, mating season, even Mitch's favorite, tax season. When did they officially begin? And why weren't they sent flyers in advance? Hugo rarely got sick, but when he did his fevers were hopeless, like the last hours of a vacation.

He pulled down his right cheek and stared at the face that long ago had stopped changing—its perfect moon shape, the eyebrows aching to become one, the translucent hairs that covered his cheeks like a kiwi. A big red pimple had made a guest appearance on the tip of his nose. He pinched it between his fingers, suddenly remembering his desire for a baby. Maybe he had morning sickness. He smiled, touching his pudgy stomach and imagining a pea-sized embryo inside. His mother used to talk obsessively about childbirth. She'd had ten children, Hugo the last. *Morning sickness was the easiest part of pregnancy,* she said once. *That queasy feeling eventually passed.*

*

Dr. Pam, a sixty-ish woman who wore little makeup and pony-tailed her matronly hair at the nape, had given Hugo smallpox vaccinations, prescribed acne medicine and Paxil, and more recently counseled him on STDs and oral sex. She had been his mother's oldest friend, and she argued with the doctors when the cancer had spread to his mother's lungs, sharing bedside shifts with Hugo and his nine siblings during the long respirator nights at the end. It was Dr. Pam whom Hugo consulted when his fever and vomiting continued and he woke from fourteen hours of sleep unable to lift himself from bed. Dr. Pam spent several examinations and three sleepless nights confirming Hugo's pregnancy. In her office she turned on a light box on the wall and showed him X-rays. "Scientifically, it's impossible, Hugo, but here, below your bladder, is clearly a womb. This round shape is the head of a developing fetus. And your blood tests repeatedly detect the presence of BhCG, a hormone found exclusively in pregnant women." Hugo listened to Dr. Pam's tempered words, finding the fluorescent X-rays both fascinating and repulsive. It was his inner organs and a fetus on display. His inner organs! And a fetus! On display! Dr. Pam wrapped her arm around his shoulders. "Congratulations, Hugo, you are the equivalent of a human platypus."

Hugo slumped in his chair. Dr. Pam smiled, offering to speak for him at a press conference. "But if you want to keep this thing under wraps, it's your decision." She clasped his hand, giving him a mock-stern look. "Miracles aside, the admiration and respect of the medical community mean nothing to me. Really, Hugo, *nada.*"

At his wastepaper basket of a desk—tucked into a corner of the busy newsroom—Hugo logged into a chat room and discovered that his frequent nosebleeds and constipation were shared by an expectant mother in Brazil. And when Mitchell wanted to have sex, Hugo caved in his chest to keep him from chafing his sensitive nipples. His family and coeditors commented on his weight gain, and as the woolly winds of October descended and he entered his second trimester, Hugo's change to oversized sweaters and snow pants seemed as ordinary as coffee with cream and sugar.

Mitchell urged him to work out. "Just do some cardio, Hugo. Twenty minutes on the bikes," he said one night as they watched Conan O'Brien banter with his fat sidekick whose name Hugo could never remember. Maybe the fat sidekick was expecting, too. How many men got pregnant each year without anyone finding out? Maybe it was some kind of cult, like Scientology. Or the breeding of mole rats.

"You don't have to lift to go to the gym," Mitchell said, kissing Hugo on the cheek before switching off the TV and turning away from him in bed. A minute passed and Hugo thought of a comeback, but Mitchell was already asleep.

Hugo realized, of course, that at some point his massive belly would no longer be concealable. During his ultrasound, a short, affable young man with dyed-blue hair (Hugo dubbed him Hefty Smurf) squeezed oily jelly on his stomach, undaunted by the fact of Hugo's pregnancy. Hefty Smurf chatted and pointed out on the monitor the fetus's doll-sized head, its salamander back, the stubs of its webby fingers. "Looks more like a weather map, doesn't it?" he said, handing Hugo a bleary photograph of the fetus. He turned off the scanning tool and wished Hugo good luck.

Hugo latched onto the happy melody of "Girlfriend in a Coma" as he left the examination room and traveled down the quiet corridors of the hospital. That was what was great about The Smiths, the way they got the combination of horror and comedy just right. He entered Dr. Pam's office, humming the bouncy tune. "You're in a devilish mood," she said.

"Pregnancy does that to a man."

He lowered himself into the corduroy chair. What was happening to him? It was as if Mother Nature had loaded up the cargo and set Hugo on a nine-month road trip. Somehow he felt less like a designated driver than a chauffeur.

Dr. Pam ran the green eraser of her pencil down a sheet in Hugo's thick medical folder. "You know, expectant mothers are prone to mood swings. Expectant *people,* I should say." Dr. Pam closed the file, her voice suddenly deepening into Serious Doctor Mode. "Let's talk game plan, Hugo. You still going to work?"

"I'm thinking of moving to the Isle of Man," he said. "I hear they offer generous paternity leaves."

He looked at Dr. Pam, who frowned at him like a wilting flower. She walked around her desk and sat in the matching corduroy chair on his left.

Hugo leaned back and crossed his legs in a figure four. It had become difficult to cross them in his usual way, feminine-like, one knee on top of the other. "I have to make money—I haven't told Mitch yet. He thinks I'm certifiable as it is."

She moved to the window, removing her scrunchie and adjusting her long white hair. "But don't you think it would be easier? I mean, if Mitch loves you . . ."

Hugo held the ultrasound photo by its corners, turning it clockwise until the hurricane pattern formed a baby. *Did Mitchell love him?* He may have been sleeping around, but Hugo considered sex a physical thing, like this pregnancy. A glint of sun from the snow outside the window made Hugo squint. Maybe love was less like the changing light in Cairo and more like his medical file, a logbook of aches and bruises that had been properly diagnosed. Hugo often thought he and Mitch were as different as butch lesbians and lipstick lesbians, but on this Mitch disagreed: he thought they complemented one another. Another time Hugo had opened a fortune cookie that said "Wisdom comes from looking backward but life must be lived forward." When Mitch balked at him, Hugo crumpled the tiny slip of paper and ate it.

Hugo thanked Dr. Pam for her concern and patted her arm, advising her to work on her doctor-patient formality. He creased the ultrasound photo in half, the glossy paper making a squeaking sound. He couldn't say it to Dr. Pam, but in his body, in the space not flooded with amniotic fluid and his small, acrobatic fetus, he believed Mitch loved him.

*

"I'm pregnant," Hugo said to Mitch at three in the morning. They were seated at the kitchen table, unable to sleep.

Mitchell drank tea and skimmed the business section of the *Globe*. "You're kidding, right?" he said flatly.

Hugo stood and walked to Mitch. "Feel." He placed Mitch's hand on his active belly.

Mitch yanked his hand away. "Jesus, Hugo! What the hell?"

"It happened the morning I threw up."

"But how—" Mitch said, one brow raised. "It's impossible." He combed his fingers through his graying cowlick. "There's no way."

"Dr. Pam confirmed it. I'm seven months along."

Hugo went to the deep metal sink and poured Mitch a glass of water. He set it on their oblong table, sliding it toward his boyfriend. Then he sat in the chair opposite Mitch, their hairy knees touching. Mitch was speechless.

Hugo thought of Dr. Pam's optimism. "Pull out the cigars, Mitch. We're having a baby."

*

Hugo was convinced the baby had a scent. It was like opening his own Starbucks: repellent to some, attracting a great many others. Joe the Intern was among those who were buying. As they put the science section to bed one Tuesday, Joe asked him if he wanted to grab a beer. Hugo had suffered two nosebleeds that day and a persistent weariness, and though his body told him to go home and rest, the thought of an empty house—Mitchell was out with friends—depressed him.

At a neon-lit sports bar, Hugo sat on a metal barstool. Joe asked the military-looking bartender for a Rolling Rock, was carded, and refused. The bartender brought Hugo a beer (what harm was one beer?) and with a conciliatory smile set a wooden bowl of peanuts in front of Joe. A drunk woman at the end of the bar gesticulated to her friend, spilling a martini. Hugo remembered the only time he'd drank a martini, in the dingy hotel bar when he'd met Mitch.

Joe grabbed a handful of nuts and watched the Bruins play on TV. They were like a pair of Before and After posters: Joe the bright-eyed student, Mitch the cynical pseudo-spouse. Why was he here with his intern, watching a hockey game in an empty bar? Was it the possibility of sex? Someone in his chat room of pregnant women had posted a message saying last trimester sex had been the best she'd ever had.

Joe turned to him. "You don't look so good, Hugo."

"I'm catching a cold."

"You've been sick a lot lately."

Hugo nodded. He drank the warm beer, hiccupping after a few sips.

Joe cleared his throat. "You live with someone, right?"

"My partner."

The freckled boy glanced at the television above Hugo's head. "The older guy? In that picture on your bulletin board?"

"His name is Mitch," Hugo said.

"So you're *gay*?" Joe whispered *gay* as if uttering the word would immediately transform him into Nathan Lane.

Hugo realized the direction of Joe's conversation. In his womb the baby did cartwheels, scratching its partially formed spine against Hugo's back. He repositioned himself on the stool. "Yes, Joe, I am gay," he said, reluctantly playing therapist. Hugo liked his self-image of the smart, young editor too hip for labels.

"Like, when did you know?" Joe asked. The boy squared himself on the stool and faced Hugo, his elbow resting on the bar.

Hugo finished his beer and asked the bartender for a glass of water. Joe ordered a Sprite. Ten years out, he tried to remember the boy's fear, that desperate feeling that hinged on whether you came out or married some hapless girl, having children and cruising public restrooms for the rest of your life. For nearly an hour Hugo shared the details of his life with Joe—the way he threw up before he came out to his mother, meeting Mitch at the conference, being out at work—and when the bartender brought them their tab, Hugo paid the bill. Then Hugo lied, asking Joe to excuse him. He said his lover was cooking omelets for them at home.

*

"The trend now is toward drugs," said Dr. Pam, her fingers intertwined on the glass desk. "Lamaze went the way of vinyl. Nowadays, moms want labor to be as easy as getting a facial."

Mitch had finally agreed to meet with Dr. Pam. They were seated in her office, separated from her by the glass desk, a sleek laptop computer, and a chrome pen-holder that looked like two lobster antennae. Hugo pressed his leg against Mitch's in the seat next to him. His getup today was a loose knee-length parka and sweatpants. Mitch was wearing chinos and a dress shirt; he had come straight from a diet consultation with a client.

Mitchell tapped his foot in measured beats on the carpet.

Dr. Pam sensed his impatience. "What's on your mind, Mitch?"

He rolled his eyes. "I'm wondering why you're entertaining Hugo's delusions."

Mitch lifted his blazer from the back of his chair and slipped into it. "Forget it. I'm going home." He stood and went to the door. When he reached for the L-shaped handle, he stopped and turned to Hugo. His face was impatient, searching.

"Are you coming?"

Hugo looked at Dr. Pam. What he wanted was to stay where he was. He longed to say to Mitch, "Sit down, listen to what Dr. Pam has to say"; what he wanted, more than anything, was for Mitch to act like an expectant father (or mother?). If pressed, he would have asked for a little peace and maybe some Louis Armstrong–wonder at the world. Instead Hugo lifted himself from the chair and took Mitch's open hand, uttering an apologetic farewell to Dr. Pam as she called his name from behind her glass desk.

*

In Hugo's daydream he was naked and also a jumbo jet. The sky was pure blue, the earth below him the crumbly texture of a cookie. He drifted slowly, idling, sailing through thin sheets of clouds. In his belly—the plane's cabin—his tropical-storm fetus pawed the walls of his stomach with its webby hands. There was something both exciting and irritating about its presence; Hugo put one arm-wing to his middle and picked at the tightened skin, as if it were a price tag he could remove if he scraped carefully.

*

"What if it's not mine?" Mitch asked that night in bed.

"What are you talking about? Of course it's yours."

"You've been sleeping around, right?"

Mitchell held the remote control, idly changing channels. Hugo was making a list of baby names: Grover, Monroe, Franklin. For some reason they kept coming out presidential. What kind of response would Milhaus receive on the jungle gym?

"How can I convince you?" Hugo asked.

"I'm throwing out questions. You always think I'm trying to sabotage you."

"It's yours, Mitch. There isn't anybody else."

"But I thought we agreed—"

"We agreed to be open. That doesn't mean I went out and screwed the first jarhead I saw."

"You mean, you haven't—?"

"With who? And when do you think I had time, between sneaking to doctor's appointments and working late on the paper?"

"But don't you want to?"

Hugo tucked his ballpoint pen behind his ear. He didn't care as much as Mitchell did about sex. Hugo placed his list of names on the milk crates. "I guess the opportunity never came up."

Mitchell turned off the TV and was silent. He rolled away from Hugo and faced the painted wall.

Hugo felt the baby kicking, the surprising jerks like desperate kernels of popcorn. He said, "It's okay, Milhaus," and rolled flat on his back, pulling the blanket to his chin.

Mitch turned and faced him. "Definitely not Milhaus," Mitch said, placing his hand gently on Hugo's stomach. "Christ. I thought only straight guys had to worry about getting their girlfriends pregnant."

*

Hugo chose a natural childbirth. The thought of pain was terrifying, but if he was going to be the first man ever to give birth, he felt a responsibility to be the first man to actually give birth, not cheat the process with an epidural like some freakish animal on a bedtable. He hired a portly midwife named Rose with a mane of Aqua Net to teach him to breathe while on his and Mitch's braided living room rug.

Now, in a breezy room overlooking the entrance of Brigham and Women's Hospital, Hugo breathed calmly. His contractions were spaced nearly ten minutes apart. He squeezed Rose's callused hand, sucking in his cheeks and saying, "This is the part of the movie where the woman starts bitching out the man."

Mitch held Hugo's other hand. He stood above Hugo, who lay on his back with knees bent on the soft opium bed.

"And the man agrees with everything," Mitch said, "because he knows that he is solely responsible for the baby, man's suffering, and, yes, all evil in the world."

Hugo smiled, the pain receding for a moment.

Dr. Pam entered and placed a hand on Mitch's shoulder. To Hugo she said, "It looks like you're doing just fine." She looked to where Rose, her friend, had pulled up a stool at the foot of the bed. "How many kids have you birthed now, Rose? It's gotta be up to fifty."

"Fifty-two. Mrs. Kaburagi gave birth to twins yesterday." Rose handed Mitch a wet towel and he dabbed it on Hugo's forehead in small swiveling gestures. "But this baby is special, I know it."

Hugo thought: special, and premature. The contractions began to quicken and Hugo could feel nothing outside his pain and the coin-sized hole in his body that this baby was struggling to get its head through. He labored in a dense fog of immediacy. For one fleeting moment he imagined his mother prostrate in this same position, the pain she had endured to give birth to him and his siblings.

Tears ran down Hugo's cheeks when the baby was born—out of joy or relief, he didn't know—and later, after she died and was placed soundlessly in his arms. They were the first moments in Hugo's life that felt real—cradling his lifeless daughter, combing her fine wet hair with his palm. Was this the experience men were never supposed to understand?

The bright April morning Hugo was released, Mitchell pushed him in a shiny wheelchair down a hospital corridor. Something about the length of the hallway reminded him of the cathedral in Cairo, its tile path for the sun embedded in the marble floor. Hugo passed an operating room with surgeons huddled in green scrubs, a waiting area with more toddlers than adults, a row of brown doors (all closed), and more operating rooms and more waiting areas. On the first floor, Mitchell pushed Hugo through the electric doors to the cracked sidewalk.

He looked up at Mitch, his house keys jangling at his waist. Aryana had asked him once what he saw in Mitchell; he'd answered something sentimental that he couldn't remember now. Mitch kissed Hugo quickly on the cheek and told him to wait while he retrieved the car.

Leaves shimmered on the maple trees around the edge of the parking lot like great green waves. A VW Bug and a bulky ambulance were idling beneath the canopy, and the people entering or leaving the hospital were bunched in groups and pairs.

Hugo wanted to revise his answer to Aryana about Mitch. I see silver-blue eyes and graying hair, he thought, pushing himself up in the wheelchair. I see sunlight fading on a cathedral floor.

ACKNOWLEDGMENTS

I would like to acknowledge the publications where these stories first appeared. "The Rice Bowl" was first published in *Memorious*; "Deaf Mute" in *The North American Review* and reprinted in the anthology *Growing Up Filipino* (Philippine American Literary House, 2003); "Nicolette and Maribel" in *Elements* and reprinted in the anthology *Walang Hiya: Literature Taking Risks Toward Liberatory Practice* (Carayan Press, 2010); "Wrestlers" in *Fifth Wednesday*; "The Foley Artist" in *Drunken Boat*; "A Visit to California" (in a slightly different form) in the anthology *Take Out: Queer Writing from Asian Pacific America* (Asian American Writers' Workshop, 2001); "Dandy" in *Post Road*; "Good Men" in *Genre*; and "Babies" in *Joyland*.

I owe a debt of gratitude—*utang ng loob*—to so many people.

This book would not have come into existence without the wonderful team at Gaudy Boy. First and foremost, Kimberley Lim, you are an exemplary editor with unwavering patience. To Judy Luo and Jia Sing Chu, thank you for your eye on reading, editing, and promoting this work. Deep appreciation to Flora Chan and Christina Newhard for exquisite book design. And to dear Jee Leong Koh, for your boundless belief in my writing—and for all that you do for Asian literature in the diaspora—I am eternally grateful. Thank you, Jee and team, for ushering this book into the world.

My teachers throughout the years taught me the pitfalls of adverbs, the marathon not the sprint, and the importance of working through endless doubt. I am indebted to Askold Melnyczuk, Alice Mattison, Rick Moody, Sven Birkerts, Liam Rector, Jill McCorkle, Betsy Cox, Allan Gurganus, Peter Ho Davies, Chinelo Okparanta, and Paul Lisicky. I have also been fortunate in the writing communities and fellowships that have supported me over the years: The Center for Fiction, Lambda Literary, the Writer's Room of Boston, Tin House Writers' Workshop, the Bennington Writing Seminars, and the Institute for Asian American Studies at California State University, Los Angeles.

To my Boston friends, thank you for making Dorchester and J. P. my home for twenty years: Alden Jones, Michael Lowenthal, Scott Heim, Jeanne Po, David Prior, Michael Kozuch, Tommy Young, Randi Triant, Andrea Graham, P. F. Potvin, Jim Faix, Christopher Kittle. I am indebted to my colleagues and friends from Boston College, where I learned the craft of teaching: in particular to Lad Tobin for taking a chance, Treseanne Ainsworth, Min Hyoung Song, Dacia Gentilella, Mary Crane, Kim Garcia, Elizabeth Graver, Suzanne Matson, Christopher Boucher, Eileen Donovan-Kranz, Rhonda Frederick, Alex Puente, Bob Chibka, Sue Roberts, Kevin Ohi, Joe Nugent, and all the amazing folks at the Learning to Learn, AHANA, FYE, and Intersections offices. To my New York friends at TC and ECFS, I have been blessed by your mentorship and friendship: Ruth Vinz, Yolanda Sealey-Ruiz, Ernest Morrell, Sheridan Blau, Bob Fecho, Tom Rock, Roger O. Anderson, Lalitha Vasudevan, Erica Walker, Felicia Mensah, Russell Marsh, Vonick Gibson,

Nayantara Mhatre, Chia-Chee Chiu, Liz J. Fernandez, Jessica Bagby, Kevin Jacobsen, Debora St. Claire, Stephanie Behrens, Katrinka Hrdy, Jason Ford, Mariama Richards, Noni Thomas Lopez, Arhm Choi Wild, Alwin Jones, Carl Anhalt, Dhari Noel, Hannah Oberman-Breindel, Michael Morse, and, of course, Gina Apostol, who was the first person to tell me about Fieldston. I was forever changed by friends from Prep for Prep: Cindy Perez, Rebecca Ervey, Michael O'Leary, and Charles Guerrero. Special shout-outs to V. Hansmann, Oona Patrick, DeLana R. A. Dameron, Shelly Oria, Ted Thompson, Heather Aimee O'Neill, Emma Straub, Julia Fierro, Ken Chen, and Nita Noveno for always creating community through literature and to Courtney Zoffness, Jane Rose Porter, and Onnesha Roydchoudhuri for rocking our fellowship year. At Kundiman, utang ng loob to Cathy, Dan, Kyle, J. Mae, Chia-Chee, Joseph, Sarah, and too many to name. To my Chadwick family in Los Angeles, Guy and I have never felt more at home and you are to thank.

I am nothing without my barkada. Whether lifting up our fellow Pinoys, marching in the streets, or just out for a night of pork and San Miguel, I am fortunate to be a part of such a strong and loving Filipino American writing community: Lara Stapleton, Gina Apostol, Nita Noveno, Marissa Aroy, Hossannah Asuncion, Sarah Gambito, Joseph O. Legaspi, R. A. Villanueva, Pat Rosal, Allison Albino, Zack Linmark, M. Evelina Galang, Bino Realuyo, Mia Alvar, Sabina Murray, Nerissa Balce, Allan Isaac, and Grace Talusan. To Jessica Hagedorn: you are generous beyond words. I am in awe to call you a friend. And I have a nice bottle of mezcal to share with you.

My family supports me and provides me with endless love and laughter. We are more than fifty Siasocos strong! From Des Moines to Minneapolis, from D. C. to Marshfield and North Carolina to Colorado, your good vibes keep me grounded and pushing for more. Witt and Holly, you have been my partners-in-crime for decades. Dianne, I love how you love and care for everyone. Jenny, you have weathered so many storms and come out stronger. To my brothers and sisters, salamat para your emotional, financial, and logistical support for so many years—I am indebted to my Kuya Sonny and Kuya Jun for always believing in me. My father, my mother, and my Kuya Jim recently passed but are always in my thoughts.

And, of course, to my husband and best friend, Guy Leavitt. What would we have done without Myspace? You are my light and love.

ABOUT THE AUTHOR

Ricco Villanueva Siasoco is a writer, educator, and activist based in Los Angeles. His work has been published in *AGNI, Joyland, Drunken Boat,* and *The North American Review.* He has received fellowships from The Center for Fiction, Lambda Literary, and the National Endowment for the Humanities. He received his MFA from Bennington College and has taught at Columbia University, Boston College, and the Massachusetts College of Art. Ricco is a board member of Kundiman, a national literary organization dedicated to Asian American literature. He is completing his EdD from Teachers College, Columbia University, where his research interests are anti-bias education, critical pedagogy, and indigenous literature. Currently, he is the Director of Equity & Inclusion at the Chadwick School in Palos Verdes.

© *Margarita Corporan*

ABOUT GAUDY BOY

From Latin *gaudium* meaning "joy," Gaudy Boy publishes books that delight readers with the various powers of art. The name is taken from the poem "Gaudy Turnout" by Singaporean author Arthur Yap, about his time abroad in Leeds, UK. Similarly inspired by such diasporic wanderings and migrations, Gaudy Boy brings literary works by authors of Asian heritage to the attention of an American audience. Established in 2018 as the imprint of the NYC-based literary nonprofit Singapore Unbound, we publish poetry, fiction, and literary nonfiction. Visit our website at www.singaporeunbound.org/gaudyboy.

Winners of the Gaudy Boy Poetry Book Prize
Autobiography of Horse by Jenifer Sang Eun Park
The Experiment of the Tropics by Lawrence Lacambra Ypil

Fiction
Malay Sketches by Alfian Sa'at

CPSIA information can be obtained
at www.ICGtesting.com
Printed in the USA
LVHW111750051119
636418LV00006B/1103/P